DOCTOR EVERYTHING

Daddy's Best Friend Romance

EMMA BLAKE

Chapter 1

Ava

I squeezed through the crowd and made it to the bar.

"Two beers, please."

Linea stopped beside me, breathless, hands on the counter, tapping her fingers. "Yes, two."

"Each?" The bartender raised a brow and looked between us.

"Yes, each. We're both thirsty and need relief," Linea deadpanned.

He got her meaning and left to fill our order.

"God, you can be so mean sometimes."

"What?" She rolled her eyes. "He asked for it."

"Just cut him some slack. We'll be needing him to fill our drink orders a lot tonight."

"Speak for yourself." Her face scrunched up. "I don't think I'll down half of one bottle."

"Let's make a bet. You'll be feeling no pain by the end of the night."

"You're on."

Four ice-cold beers were placed on the counter, and we each grabbed two.

"I'll show you, Ava," she told me, then said to the bartender, "Thank you."

I surveyed the crowd, eyes out for a booth.

"See? He smiled at me. I'm nice."

"I didn't see it."

"Should I go sweet-talk him again? You have to watch this time."

"Or we could grab the booth that just emptied." I nodded to the space a couple had just left.

"Yes!" Linea raced ahead. "Go, go, go."

She slid in first, and I quickly followed her lead.

We both giggled and thumped our beers onto the smooth polished table.

"That's the biggest win I've had today."

"You say that about everything." I shook my head, a smile curving my lips. "Finishing the cleaning in Ramona's kitchen, snagging the last piece of cake she left out…"

"What can I say? I'm always winning." Linea shrugged off her coat, running her fingers through her honey-blonde hair, wet from the rain. Water droplets fell on my face.

I put out a hand. "Watch it."

She laughed.

I unwrapped my scarf and my own damp hair touched my bare neck. "Argh." I shivered and shook out my hair.

Linea yelled and scooched far away from me, giving me a disapproving look.

Laughing, I picked up my drink and swallowed a mouthful.

My gaze skated around the room. Busters was a beehive this Friday night. It seemed everyone had clocked out after the work week ended and decided this was their favorite way to wind down.

It definitely was mine. Every few weekends, Linea and I showed up, had a few beers, and relaxed. Not that the karaoke singer's rendition of "Poker Face" was providing any form of relaxation.

"What is that?" Linea frowned and faced the stage.

The guy was in his element. He strutted across the stage, tossing his non-existent long hair over his shoulder.

"The diva we didn't know we needed."

My friend laughed and shook her head. "I want to go up there and tell him to stop. I've had a long week. He's ruining my evening."

"Don't." I eyed her.

"I won't."

Keeping my eyes on her, I sipped my beer.

Linea chuckled. "So, about next week's schedule…"

"What? No. It's the weekend, Linea, no shoptalk."

Linea and I ran our own business, cleaning homes for a living. We loved helping others by creating spick-and-span, organized havens for them. It was fulfilling and fun working with my best friend. But it also bled into after-work hours.

"Fine." She raised both hands and shrugged.

Linea grabbed her phone, and blue light illuminated her face. I slid lower in the booth, blew out a breath, and shot a gaze around. I could name almost every face my eyes connected with, and a couple waved. I waved back.

Lively chatter rang out around me. I could easily start up a conversation with anyone while my best friend was snapping different angles of her face to post selfies on Instagram. But chatting with the same people was all I ever did.

Every day, the same routine. Clean houses. See the same faces. Visit our hometown bar.

I loved living in a small town; I really did. But lately I'd been…bored. I just wanted something different. Anything at all to spice up my life. But in Hannibal, that was too much to hope for.

Or was it?

My eyes fell on the entrance just as a man walked in. Unlike those making up the typical crowd at Busters, he was dressed to the nines. A black suit clung to his tall frame, and a dark blue tie ran down the front of the white button-down underneath.

I tilted my head, trying to make out his features. His face was turned down, concentration fixed on his black umbrella. With long deft fingers, he fastened the tie wrap. Lucky umbrella.

Then his gaze lifted.

My heart clenched.

Deep gray eyes set in a rugged, strong face took in the room. Those stormy eyes bounced off me, and my breath caught. A sensation snaked through my belly—something foreign and delicious.

His gaze fixed on the bar, and his body followed. Lean strength sparked through with every measured step he took.

He dropped lithely onto a bar stool, his back to the booths. I shook myself out of my trance, glancing around. I'd lost myself there for a minute.

Judging by the ladies turned in his direction, I wasn't alone. All but Linea. She was still focused on her phone. I elbowed her and nodded to the man.

She leaned over, trying to make out his face. "Oh my." She sat back. "Who's that silver fox?"

"Hell if I know." My words came out a little breathless.

Linea gave no indication she noticed, her eyes still on the man. "But really. Who is he? Where did he come from? That face is hard to forget."

More than his face. The energy surrounding him was potent, crackling like electricity. My body thrummed, wanting to tap into that power.

"Someone new? A visitor?"

"Probably," I muttered, then sipped my beer. My insides were still recovering.

Someone new. It clicked. Different from all the people I knew—and loved—but hell, I knew them all too well.

I didn't need to think about it. I should, instead, follow my instincts. How many times did breathtaking strangers show up in Hannibal?

This was the universe deciding I deserved a good time. Just one night to forget my humdrum life. I'd never before had a one-night stand. It was something every confident woman should experience once in her life, right? My girly bits agreed, aching to be touched by those skillful-looking hands that were now nursing a beer.

I swallowed. He was what I needed.

He'd be a break from the same old same old. A breath of fresh air.

I wanted—no, needed—that fresh air. One night of hot, meaningless sex. The memories would last me a lifetime.

A shiver tingled up my spine, my nerves jumping. I was doing this. No turning back now.

I was going to hit on a handsome stranger.

Whatever resulted, *stranger* was the key word. A no strings attached, fun night. And if the sex was terrible, I'd never see him again, so it didn't matter.

"How many seconds until someone walks up to him?" Linea's gaze flitted around the bar.

I fluffed out my hair. "Five seconds."

"What?" My friend turned. "I was thinking they'd let

him have at least one drink… Oh." Linea's eyes skimmed my body. "Undo one button. No, two."

I did as she asked. "Okay?"

"Mm-hmm." She drained her bottle.

"Wish me a win." I tossed her my scarf. It'd get in the way of my sexy look.

"May my winnings be with you." Linea raised her empty bottle. "Gosh, I need another."

Smiling at my friend, I slid the strap of my bag over my shoulder and started out of the booth. She followed suit. But as I headed for the bar, she dove into the next booth. A chorus of "hey" rang out behind me as our friends greeted Linea.

I paid them no mind, all my attention glued to the stranger's strong back. While others hunched over their drinks, he sat up straight, with perfect posture.

An image flashed through my head of my nails raking down his back. I bet his backside was muscular and taut. Fit for grabbing onto while he pumped between my thighs.

Said legs turned to jelly the closer I got. I took a deep breath, shaking out my hair and relaxing my shoulders. So what if I scrubbed floors for a living? And in contrast, this hot, hunky stranger looked like he could grace the cover of *GQ*?

None of it mattered. We wouldn't exchange anything beyond the physical. We could be a one-night distraction for each other, satisfying our animalistic needs.

I reached the stool next to him in two strides and slid onto it. The only indication he noticed my existence was the slight tick of his jaw. It relaxed as he resumed staring at his drink.

That gave me an opportunity to really look. His sharp features—high cheekbones and a strong jawline—were softened by full lips and long lashes. His salt and pepper hair was pushed back from his forehead, faded at the edges, and fuller on top. I slid a discreet gaze to his finger. No ring or ring outline.

My eyes lingered on his long fingers, and I swallowed. I wanted those hands on me.

"Hey." My voice came out smoky and low, despite my nerves. Win!

The man side-eyed me.

Oh, shit. My stomach pooled with liquid heat from only a look.

Just that glance made me want to either shrink away or rub up against him. "You're not from around here," I continued, inwardly cringing at my cheesy pickup line.

His face turned to me now, brow raised. "What?"

Goosebumps skittered up my arms at his smooth, deep baritone. I wasn't sure where I found the voice to continue speaking. "I know nearly every face in Hannibal. You're not from around here."

"So?" His full brow arched higher, gray eyes rivaling the stormy skies outside.

I resisted the urge to stammer and forged on. He could just be at the end of a bad day. A little friendliness would help him loosen up. "You're new, all alone. I could keep you company."

His eyes ran down my body, pausing on my exposed cleavage. His throat worked for a second before his gaze lifted to my face. "No, thanks."

His cold words doused the heat running through my veins. And yet...for a second, he looked ready to take me up on my offer.

Tossing my hair, I smiled. "Aww, come on. Everyone says I'm good company."

"So go and keep everyone else company."

"They're not hanging out at a bar all alone on a Friday night."

He sighed, looking away from me. Instead of showing interest, it seemed I annoyed him. Was I so dull? A sinking feeling crowded in my belly. I looked behind me and spotted Linea. She waved, then gave me an enthusiastic thumbs-up.

I turned back to the man with a slightly boosted confidence. "So, would you like to buy me a drink?" I leaned forward on my elbow. His eyes ate me up once more, and I smiled. "That's the decent thing to do."

He tore his gaze from me, eyes back to his drink. "Maybe you should leave; that'd be the decent thing to do."

I sat back, my face flaming. I opened my mouth and shut it. No witty comeback came to mind.

There was no fun spin I could put on his words. He had rejected me. Clearly.

I hopped off the stool, hands wrapped around my bag strap. I looked toward Linea, but she was caught up in cheering on the next karaoke singer, who was doing a great job. Keeping my head down, I headed for the exit.

Rain plastered my hair to my face and my clothes to my skin. But I kept my face down and walked, determined to get home and forget my embarrassing encounter tonight.

Why had I thought I could be a sexy temptress and lure a sophisticated man like him in? I was just boring old Ava. And getting soaked in the pouring rain was what I got for stepping out of my comfort zone.

Suddenly, the rain stopped. I brought my head up. No, it hadn't stopped. It was still falling *around* me, but not *on* me because...someone was holding an umbrella.

I turned, and my gaze met gray eyes. I took a step

back, moving back under the rainfall. "What do you want?" I eyed the man.

He looked at the empty road before meeting my eyes. "I was being a jerk earlier." He lowered his head, like the thought embarrassed him. Then his gaze met mine again. "Share my umbrella and let me walk you home."

I started to say no, but he cut in.

"It's the decent thing to do."

A small thrill zinged through me that he used my quip from earlier. "Fine."

Something that was not quite a smile passed across his face.

We huddled underneath the umbrella as we started off. Not the way I'd hoped the night would go. But the warmth from his body was welcome.

Chapter 2

Liam

She remained silent on the walk home. Unsurprisingly so, since I shut down her earlier attempts. I was an asshole going off on her that way.

But it was intentional and for good reason.

Years of working with no downtime left no opportunities for socializing. Any break in my routine to take time off resulted in—you guessed it—more work.

Coming to Hannibal gave me a glimpse of life outside my normally busy schedule. I thought I'd hit a bar on my Friday night off. Only to have a stunning chestnut-haired goddess show up.

If I engaged in conversation with her, it wouldn't take five sentences for her to realize I sucked at flirting. Better to chase her away with my rude attitude than bear the embarrassment afterward. I thought I'd annoy her so she would move on.

What I didn't anticipate was how the hurt in her eyes would affect me. Then, her storming out into the rain caused me to worry for her well-being. I barely knew this gorgeous woman, and I already wanted to keep her safe.

She shivered now and wrapped her arms around her middle. Her shoulders folded in as if to protect her body from the chill. If only I could protect her more.

The umbrella managed to keep the worst of it away. But the rain blew in every direction, still hitting her, molding her clothes to her body.

I was drenched, too, but thought nothing of it. My body was too attuned to her pressing close to get some relief from the rain. And my eyes kept slipping to the curve of her ass in those tight black jeans.

She took a left turn onto the next street. "We're close."

My head whipped up. It was a busy street. Stores lined the road on both sides, some closed, others still open. But outside, only a few people huddled underneath umbrellas like us.

A short walk brought us to an adjoined coffee shop and bakery.

"Home sweet home." Her voice was light and airy.

I frowned. "You live in the shop?"

She laughed. "No, above it." Her gaze rose and I followed it.

A small balcony hung over the store signs. Potted plants and flowers decorated it. A glass double door led out onto the balcony. Beyond that, it was dark inside.

"Come on up." She nodded toward the spiral staircase. "We're soaked. I'll get you a towel, and maybe some tea to warm you up."

Before I could answer, her feet hit the first rung. Closing the umbrella, I followed.

I tried to avert my eyes, but her ass looked good enough to bite. Or grab with my hands as she rode my cock.

"We're here." She stopped by her front door and fished out keys from her purse.

Her hands shook a little as she slid the key in. Was it from the cold or my presence? If it was the latter, her chirpy "Come on in" gave no indication.

I left the dripping umbrella by the door and walked in.

"I'll get the towels," she announced, disappearing behind a door at the far end of the living room.

I looked around the room while I waited for my temptress to return. One long couch and a one-seater was all it could carry. They faced a flat screen TV hung up on the wall and a low coffee table tied it all together. Plants were scattered around in what little space remained.

I worked off my jacket and hung it on the coat rack. My eyes just took in the kitchenette in one sweep when she returned.

"Here are the—" she paused, eyes roaming over my upper body. Her gaze darkened and her tongue ran across her lower lip "—towels."

She stood glued in one spot, staring. A small smile played on my lips.

Closing the gap between us, I took one. "Thanks."

She blinked. "Of course." Turning away, she wrapped the towel around her hair.

I ran the towel through my own hair. I wouldn't truly be dry unless I got out of my clothes. Best to stop the wet tendrils from dripping down my face.

My hair was as dry as I could get it when I lowered my hands. My eyes caught on her. She was still drying her hair, hands lifted, making her wet top strain over her chest.

Those luscious tits tempted a groan from my throat. Just a taste. Her nipples stood hard and erect, begging to be licked.

The desire to suck one into my mouth was like a vise

clutching my throat. I wanted to nibble on it, roll my tongue around the bud until she was panting.

She dropped her hands and shook out her hair, her chest shaking along with it.

Fuck me.

A strangled moan escaped my mouth.

Her eyes connected with mine then, lips parting. The towel slipped from her fingers, hitting the floor. Her chest rose and fell rapidly, throat dipping as she swallowed.

"So, um, about that tea..." She licked her lips. "What kind do you like?"

Tea? What was she talking about? The only thing I wanted on my tongue was the heat between her thighs.

"You know this isn't about tea." My voice came out gruff.

Her face flushed as she whispered, "And you didn't want to just walk me home."

I shook my head.

That small admission broke the invisible wall between us. She reached out, wrapping her arms around my neck. My hands went to her hips and I pulled her close, so her core was pressed against mine.

A small gasp left her lips just as our mouths crashed together. The taste of her fruity lip gloss burst on my tongue as I sucked on her lower lip. She moaned, yanking me down for a deeper kiss. And I was more than happy to oblige.

Stroking my tongue along her lips, I pried them open, licking into her mouth. A growl ripped through my chest. Her taste was intoxicating.

Her response was a breathless moan, hands skimming my back, then around to my chest. Her fingers fumbled. I drew back long enough so she could loosen my tie.

Our lips came together again, our tongues tangling.

Even with the distraction of her silky mouth on mine, I found the edge of her top easily. We broke apart so I could pull it off.

She slipped my tie off immediately after. Working to undo my buttons took a bit longer, and she let out a frustrated huff. I chuckled, assisting her until we'd removed my dress shirt.

When my undershirt came off, her gaze rode greedily up my chest and back down. Her eyes widened, glued to the outline of my cock straining against my zipper.

"You'll have *that* in a minute," I murmured, cupping her face and kissing her again.

She pressed against me once more. This time, the heat from her skin melted into me. Caressing her soft skin, I made my way to the nipples that had tortured me all night.

Her whimper sent blood rushing to my cock. I wanted to be locked inside her when she made that sound.

"Bedroom," she said between fevered kisses.

We hustled to the door she'd gone through before. As she broke off to unbuckle my pants, my gaze flitted around and caught a high mattress, and yet again, more plants in the cozy space.

But nothing could hold my attention for more than a second. A brown-haired beauty was standing before me, eyes shining as she stroked her fingers in the waistband of my briefs.

She worked them off and my hard cock bounced free. Her gaze followed the motion and locked on the head. It shone with precum.

Her eager tongue swiped her lower lip and she raised a hand. Feverish excitement slithered through me and my dick throbbed harder. If she so much as touched me, this would be over before it began.

I stepped out of her reach to rid myself of the pants around my legs, along with my shoes and socks.

"Your turn." I stalked over to her.

Wide eyes went from my body to my face. I kissed her deeply, then gently pushed her back to the bed. I undid her jeans button and slid the zipper down.

She assisted as I tugged her jeans down. I intended to take it all off so she would be laid bare before me. But halfway there, getting a glimpse of the bare mound at the apex of her thighs, coupled with her sweet aroma reaching my nostrils, forced me to abandon my mission.

I pressed my face to that spot and inhaled. She gasped, her hand gathering a fistful of my hair. I darted my tongue out for a quick taste before I resumed taking the jeans off all the way.

But the musky flavor on my tongue had me ravenous. I eased her down and parted her knees. My tongue met her clit, and her back arched off the bed, her body pressing into my face.

"More, please," she whimpered.

Her pleasured cry sent purpose flooding through me. I found a rhythm with my tongue that kept her panting. Then I worked my middle finger between her damp folds.

"Oh God," she screamed, rocking against my face.

My cock jerked, demanding to be buried in her eager pussy. But I was determined to bring her pleasure first.

With a low growl, I slipped my finger into her channel. Her heat engulfed me, her wetness dripping down my hand.

Curving my finger, I found her pleasure spot and stroked. She responded with a twist of her hips, riding my finger and my face. I slipped a second finger in, and sucked her clit between my lips.

Her legs shook and tightened around my head.

"Oh, oh. I'm coming. I'm—" Her words turned into a low whine and she clenched around my fingers.

I groaned and licked her, over and over again, absorbing the shocks of her trembling. I only pulled away when she sagged back down on the bed.

Aftershocks trembled through her body and she ran her hands through her hair.

"That was amazing." She exhaled, smiling.

Her eyes met mine, tracked down to my cock, and turned heavy-lidded. She kicked off her jeans, then knee-walked to me.

Slim fingers wrapped around my shaft and I bucked. A curse tore from my lips. She quickly silenced it with a kiss, and as I groaned, she deepened it.

Her grip tightened, moving faster.

"I have to fuck you now." I broke away from our kiss. "On your back."

Breathlessly, she obeyed. My eyes dragged up her body, unable to look away from her perfect pussy, soft skin, and mouthwatering breasts.

But my dick demanded more.

I covered her body with mine, lining up my cock with her core. A gasp escaped her lips and her eyes fell shut as I entered her. I rocked forward and her hips rose, meeting mine, thrust for thrust.

I stared down at her. An angel with her hair haloing around her face, lips parted with pleasure, tits jiggling with each stroke.

Leaning down to kiss her lips, I raised my hips and pulled out slowly, dragging my cock along her walls, leaving just the head inside.

I swallowed her protest, which quickly turned to a moan as I pushed back inside her.

"Fuck," I groaned. "I want to make this good, but—" I

pulled back out and drove in again. "Fuck, you feel so good."

She let out a cry, hands clutched around my back, nails raking down my spine. "Don't stop. Keep going."

Burying my face against her shoulder, I hooked a hand behind her knee and lifted her leg while driving into her. Over and over. She took my quick, harried fucking with soft moans, begging me for more.

Harder. Don't stop. Oh God, I'm coming.

I leaned back and took in her knotted forehead. She was coming, even though I was jackhammering into her? But she did.

Her snug wetness gripped me so tight, I came, too. A growl tore from my throat as I managed two more thrusts before I buried myself in her.

I gave into the pleasure coursing through me. Kissed her as the last tremors thrummed through us.

Her hands tracked up to my hair. Kept me pinned there until we broke off breathlessly.

Then she hit me with a blinding smile. "Wow."

"What?" I was still catching my breath.

"Oh, um, nothing."

I fell onto my side and pulled her against me. For some reason, I wanted to keep feeling her skin against mine.

This would end tonight. I might as well make the pleasure last.

"I don't even know your name," she muttered, snuggling against me.

I chuckled and stroked her hair. "Doesn't matter."

Once she fell asleep, I would be gone.

Chapter 3

Ava

I rang the doorbell at Dad's house and waited.

The door slammed open. "Ava!" Dad barreled out and swept me up in a bear hug.

"Dad, don't—" Air snuffed out of my lungs as he squeezed me tight.

He grinned and butterfly-kissed my cheek. A reluctant smile pulled at my lips. His hug probably cracked my back in five places, but it was snuggly and warm, so I allowed it.

"How are you, Peanut?" He dropped me, ruffling my hair.

This was the drill whenever I came over for Sunday dinners. I gave up styling my hair and simply opted for ponytails. Dad's many hugs and head rubs left me looking like I'd been buzzed with static electricity.

"I'm fine, Dad." I ran my free hand through my hair. "You're as cheerful as ever."

His always-smiling brown eyes crinkled at the corners. "You know it."

"Here." I handed him the paper bag that had somehow survived his tackling hug.

Dad took it and peeked in. "Cake," he exhaled. "Did you make this?"

"I wish. I got it from the bakery beneath my unit."

He laughed. "Classic Ava. Come on in."

He stepped back, and I slipped past his imposing build into my childhood home. Everything was warm-toned, cream and brown, with the occasional pop of an orange color Dad loved. The familiar space felt different today.

"Have you done something new with the place?" I shrugged off my jacket and hung it up.

"Nah, nothing really." Dad shut the door. "Unless you count this new contemporary art piece!"

He rushed to the mantel, doing a Vanna White hand gesture.

My gaze skipped over the photos and keepsakes to the newest addition.

I gasped, hurrying to his side. The mini statue was shaped like a bee, but with the head of a woman. "The lady and the bee! You've always wanted it."

"And now I've got it." Dad stared at it, eyes soft. "Isn't it glorious?"

"It is. How did you get it?"

"I may have promised Sonnie six months' worth of cereal in return."

"Dad," I chuckled. "You always trade groceries for goods."

He ran a successful grocery store and could afford it. But still.

"What? I don't always do that." His eyes rolled up and he pressed his lips together. "Well, maybe. This time was for my heart's desire."

I shook my head, still smiling. "Good for you, then."

"Better on me." Dad grabbed my hand. "I've never felt so alive. I'm trying new things. Like this recipe I saw online."

He tugged my arm and I flinched.

"Are you okay?" Dad dropped my hand and turned concerned brown eyes on me.

Two nights ago, I had mind-blowing sex with a stranger, and now I'm sore in places I didn't know I could be, I thought, keeping it to myself. Instead, I responded, "Yes?"

"Hmm." He swept a disbelieving gaze over me.

"Come on, Dad." I bumped his shoulder. "Tell me about your new recipe!"

"Oh, yes." He jumped into action and I shuffled after him.

My schedule confirmed three homes to clean tomorrow. It would be a challenge at work. Every step I took revealed stiff muscles.

It was worth it, though. Fantastic sex with a handsome stranger was what I'd needed—and got. I'd had my once-in-a-lifetime, wild, carefree night that I could remember forever.

Even if it meant dealing with a few aches and pains. At least they came with the memory of a pleasurable night nothing could top.

"Ava?"

"What?" I blinked.

"You're standing there, smiling into space." A line had formed between my dad's brows.

"Oh, don't mind me." I hurried into the kitchen, smiling to hide my wince. "I'm just enjoying the aromas."

Indeed, everything smelled delicious. My stomach growled in response. Dad was a cook like no other.

"I didn't always know how to cook. If your mom could see me now, she would be so proud," he often used to say.

Mom died when I was really young, so Dad and his amazing meals were all I knew.

"I made avocado soup for the starter, chicken casserole with roasted broccoli as a main, and for dessert—" he pulled out a glass container from the fridge and lifted it toward me "—creamy chocolate mousse."

I could almost hear choirs singing with rays beaming from the sky to light it up.

"Ooh…" My voice tapered out. "What makes this different from all the other chocolate mousses we've had?"

Dad grinned. "Don't worry, you'll see. It's a fresh new ingredient."

"Jeez, Dad, don't tell me you put a vegetable in it."

"What? No." He placed his prized mousse back in the fridge. "It's sweet, I promise."

The dining table was covered in so much food. It was always a lot when Dad cooked, but tonight, it was two times the usual amount. My eyes narrowed.

"Dad, are we having a—"

The doorbell rang.

"Oh, Peanut, I forgot to tell you. We're having a guest." He started taking off his apron.

"Dad, what guest?" I eyed him, a smile on my face.

"No, it's not a woman."

"So, it's a man?" I gasped, brow raised. "You never told me."

"Ava!" He went red in the face. "It's not what you think."

I grinned. "Really? What am I thinking?"

He rolled his eyes. "It's just a friend from out of town who's visiting."

"A friend. How cryptic."

Dad rumbled an annoyed sound, his brows pulled down. He started speaking, but the doorbell rang again.

"Dad, don't keep your friend waiting." I reached a finger into the casserole, but Dad slapped my hand. "Ow."

"Don't touch anything. Tonight has to be perfect."

"For your friend?" I nursed the back of my hand with a rub but still managed to wiggle my brows.

He huffed something about a smart aleck-y daughter but headed off. It was always fun messing with him.

My gaze fell back to the table and my mouth watered. I threw a glance at the archway that led to the kitchen. Dad's booming voice sounded as he welcomed his guest.

That should take a while.

I picked at the steaming casserole in the middle of the table and snagged a piece of chicken. Score! That'd tide me over until Dad and his guest returned.

It was definitely a date. He was just too shy to admit it.

"And here's my daughter, Ava," Dad announced behind me.

I swallowed and turned in one quick motion. "I wasn't touching the food!"

My eyes met gray ones as they narrowed and my breath caught. What the hell was stormy stranger doing in my dad's house? "You…" I trailed off, unable to speak.

Not because I was too stunned. Something was in my throat. I couldn't breathe.

I was choking.

My hands clutched at my throat, chest heaving.

"Ava, are you okay?"

"Dad…" I wheezed, bending over and coughing, my eyes watering.

My hacking failed to dislodge the lump. It hurt so bad.

Somewhere in the distance, Dad yelled, "Help her!"

I tried to speak, but my entire being just wanted to breathe.

Strong arms wrapped around my middle, and a body covered mine from behind.

Losing breath...

The arms around me squeezed and my ribs dug into my side. The pain barely registered. I just needed air.

Another squeeze and the lump moved. On the third squeeze, the food dislodged. It flew out of my mouth and across the room.

Dad ducked in time to avoid it. "Ava." He collected me in his arms. "You okay?"

I took in gulping breaths as I shook. "I'm fine."

"Jesus, Peanut. Next time pinch something you can swallow on short notice."

"I didn't."

Dad eyed me.

Sighing, I mumbled, "Okay."

"Liam, thank God you were here." Dad looked behind me.

I froze and bit my lip. He was really here.

"It's no problem, Thomas. Choking is quite common. Helps to know the Heimlich maneuver."

This cannot be happening. My wild hook-up was supposed to remain anonymous. Now he was at my dad's house. And how did he make the word "choking" sound so sexy?

"Not in this house, it's not," Dad replied. "But I should learn to do that instead of screaming like a banshee the next time."

Dad shared a laugh with his friend. Liam. Oh my God. I could put a name to his face in my head now.

What happened to good old anonymity and one-night stands?

Dad would find out. He'd be mad, and I'd—

"Ava, say hi to Liam. He's the friend I told you about."

Forcing myself not to cringe, I inched my way around to face Liam.

As on Friday night, he wore a button-down and black pants with dress shoes. This time, there was no tie. Just two buttons cracked open to reveal tanned skin.

My cheeks flamed and my gaze shot up to his face. He was assessing me just as I was him.

His dark brows were a bit drawn over gray eyes that looked like a storm ready to unleash its power. High cheek-bones. Full, sensual lips that had gone down on me two nights ago.

"Hi." My voice came out choked, my heart rate spiking.

"Jesus, I forgot. You need water." Dad scrambled behind me and produced a glass. "Drink."

I collected it and chugged, avoiding Liam's eyes.

"Come on. Come sit." Dad herded me to my spot at the table.

I dropped into the chair and drained the glass.

"You need more?"

Before I could answer, Dad collected the glass. I offered him a thankful smile. The moment his steps receded, I threw a glance behind me to make sure he was truly gone.

Then I leaned forward. "You're my Dad's friend?" I hissed at Liam, who sat across from me.

His shoulders moved carelessly, brow lifted. "So?"

"So?" My eyes bulged. "So?" He couldn't be serious. "If he finds out what happened between us on Friday night..."

"I wasn't going to tell him," he said. "Were you?"

"Uh, no." I sat back and thought for a second. "Did you know?"

"That you were my friend's daughter before I fucked you?"

A thrill traveled up my spine. "You don't need to spell it out."

"No, I didn't know who you were."

His tone said he wouldn't have touched me if he'd known. But his eyes were saying he'd do it again.

My body heated with the latter observation. I pressed my thighs together and clenched my teeth at the sensation in my core. It could never happen again.

"Fine," I bit out. "He can never find out. Ever."

"Ava," Dad said behind me, incredibly close.

I whipped around, heart hammering. "Yes?" Did he hear us?

"You'll never guess what I found out."

I gulped, my throat suddenly dry. "What?"

Chapter 4

Liam

"Lemon water clears your throat." Thomas handed his daughter the water. "Drink up."

Her tense shoulders loosened and I could almost see the relief rolling off her.

"Thanks, Dad." She took a sip, grimaced, then set it aside. "I think I'm fine now."

"So, where were we?" Thomas dropped into the chair at the head of the table. "Let's try this again. Ava, Liam Cooper, my friend." He stressed the last word, and a small smile ticked her lip up. "And Liam, my daughter, my Peanut—"

"Dad." She rolled her eyes.

"—Ava Morellis."

"Nice to meet you, Ava." I looked across the table, noticing the freckles lightly scattered across her face.

Her cheeks blushed pink, and she ducked her head. "Nice to meet you, too, Liam."

"What a way to meet for the first time, huh?" Thomas

laughed. "Choking on a piece of chicken."

Ava laughed an airy sound. "Yep, first meeting."

She was so damn nervous and jittery, unable to sit still. Thomas was clueless. Why was she so worried?

Her eyes flicked so fast between her dad and me that she should've been dizzy by now.

"Let's eat."

Ava rushed to pick up the ladle and dish herself some soup. Her hands shook a bit, spilling some.

"Can I help?"

Her brown eyes pinned me with a murderous look. "I can take care of it myself."

"Liam is a medical doctor," Thomas supplied. "They have to have steady hands for their job. Or are those surgeons? Anyway, Liam is the best doctor I know. If you're still shaken about the choking, he can assist you."

"You're very generous with the praise, Thomas." I stood and took the ladle.

She let it go quickly so our skin didn't touch. Shame.

"But I do have good hands, indeed." I smiled.

Ava huffed and picked up her spoon, holding it like a weapon.

Swallowing my chuckle, I topped up her soup and dished for myself and Thomas.

As we settled to eat, Thomas spoke. "So, tell me, what have you been up to? How do you like Hannibal?"

"It's great so far. I went to Busters the other night."

A clang came from Ava's end.

"You okay, Peanut?" Thomas turned to her.

"Fine, just fine," she bit out.

When he faced me once more, she threw a dark warning look my way.

I reined in my smile. "It was a nice place. After a

couple of drinks, I went home. Didn't have that much time to kick back and relax when I was in the city."

My friend's features creased sympathetically. "Hannibal moves at a much slower pace. You'll like it here."

"You're staying?" Ava gaped.

"For the time being, yes."

She stared at me wide-eyed.

"Liam moved into an old house that belonged to his family. He plans to set up his practice there." He poked his daughter's shoulder. "Wouldn't that be awesome? Another great medical doctor to help the folks of Hannibal."

"Awesome," Ava said flatly and filled her mouth with a spoonful of soup.

Thomas missed his daughter's discomfort and went on about how great I was for Hannibal. Hannibal was great for me, too. Well, that was, until I discovered Ava's identity.

Still, I wasn't upset. Unlike the fiery princess whose eyes kept spitting fire at me. Granted, I earned that with my teasing.

Her dad turned away to take another helping of the chicken casserole. Which was exquisite, no argument there. I held two fingers to my lips and made a closing zipper motion.

Those brown eyes sparkled and I bit back a chuckle.

Enchanting girl.

I should probably be bothered that I slept with Thomas's daughter. If my math was correct, I had about eighteen years on her.

But I didn't know it at the time, and she was a grown woman. Knowing now, though, changed nothing.

The only thing her brown eyes managed to arouse in me was desire. So acute that if someone spilled hot soup on themselves, I couldn't stand up to help. I was rock-hard under the table.

I'd thought about her the past couple of days. Certain we'd never meet again. But seeing her here was a gift.

Perks of small-town life.

Shame she was my friend's daughter. Or was it, really?

We could have a go between the sheets again. It'd be our little secret.

Our eyes caught and hers narrowed like she could read my mind.

"Liam, know what else is great for Hannibal?"

I shook my head as reality came into focus. Shit, I'd been staring openly at Ava. "No, Thomas, what's that?"

"Why, the Second Chance Restaurant. You should see the folks who come from out of town to eat there."

"Interesting. Are the owners residents?"

"Yes, Cal and Allie, right?" He nodded at Ava and she returned a quick one. "Ava grew up with Allie. Well, around her. She was two grades behind the young woman. What a life." He sighed. "The kids are the future, I'm telling you."

Young woman.

That's what Ava was. Too young for me.

I shouldn't be doing this—wanting to fuck my friend's daughter.

My oldest and closest friend. I couldn't do that to him.

I lifted my gaze to her. Her brown hair had come loose from her ponytail, tumbling around her shoulders. A soft lock dropped between her cleavage and rested on her left breast.

My fingers tightened around my spoon. Compared to my forty-two years, she was young, but damn, did my body refuse to accept it.

Those tempting eyes met mine as she spooned choco-late mousse into her mouth. My cock jerked. I wanted those lips wrapped around my dick.

And there went my regret.

After dinner, Thomas shooed me out of the kitchen so he and Ava could clean up.

I spent the time perusing their photos, and was that a bee? Or a woman? I shook my head and went to the next picture.

Ava was a teen here. Face flushed as she knelt by a tub with another girl around the same age. Their arms wrapped around a big wet dog.

"Charity dog wash for the orphanage," Thomas said behind me.

"That's lovely." I faced him. "You must be proud."

"More than proud." He sighed, massive shoulders deflating. "At only twenty-four, the things she's done... I wish her mom could see her now. The woman she's become."

"Dad." Ava popped into the living room. "Do you have a casserole for me?"

"Sure thing, Peanut. I'll get it."

I frowned. Didn't we just eat? Or did she want leftovers?

Thomas left and returned with a large pan. "Here you go."

A big smile curved her lips. The most genuine she'd displayed all night.

She collected the offering and peeked in before sliding the lid back in place. "Thanks, Dad. The Mullens family could really use it."

"It's alright, Peanut." Thomas ruffled her hair.

"Ugh, Dad!" Ava complained, but laughed good-naturedly. "Will you ever stop?"

"Only when these hands stop moving." He started for a head rub again but she skipped out of the way, racing for the door.

Thomas's booming laughter followed, and warmth ignited in my chest.

We were out the door, standing on the porch, when Thomas spoke again. "Liam, it was wonderful having you over. We should do this often."

Ava stiffened beside me.

I smiled at my friend, regardless. "Thank you. Dinner was lovely."

"Will you make sure Ava makes it home safely?" Thomas cast a pointed gaze around the dark yard and curb. "She didn't bring her car again, I see."

"It was a lovely evening. I just wanted to walk," she said.

"And now it's a dark night."

"Come on, we both know nothing dangerous happens in Hannibal. You're being dramatic."

"Dramatic is how I'd react if I saw something had happened to you on the morning news." Thomas turned to me. "Please, take her home. And pass by the Mullens house so she can—"

"Dad, hello! I'm right here and I can take care of myself. I'm a grown woman. And it's a lovely night to enjoy a walk. It'll take only twenty minutes."

"Twenty minutes is long enough for something to happen to you, Peanut." He ruffled her hair. "Now, let Liam take you home."

"Dad, I—"

"Ava…"

"Don't worry, Thomas. I won't let her out of my sight." I wrapped an arm around her shoulder for good measure. "Come on, Ava."

She threw a glare at me, but my attention was on Thomas's huge smile.

"Thanks, Liam. Goodnight."

I sent a "goodnight" over my shoulder as I herded her to the car.

"Don't let any of this go to your head," she hissed, tearing herself from my side.

Smiling, I pulled open the car door. "It's not, I promise."

She huffed an annoyed sound before looking toward the porch, smiling sweetly. "Goodnight, Dad."

He waved back.

Thomas only went back indoors when the car moved down the driveway.

In the car's interior, Ava was a statue beside me. She clutched the casserole pan with white-knuckled fingers, her mouth pressed shut.

A kiss would soften them for sure.

I turned into the next street. Where had that thought come from? I shook my head to clear it.

It was amusing when I pushed her buttons at dinner. Now, though, dinner was behind us, and I was done teasing.

"Where's the Mullens' home?"

Her directions came out in a clipped tone.

I gritted my teeth and drove. Soon, we stopped outside a suburban house.

The fog around Ava lifted. She hopped out of the car. "I'll be right back."

A quick walk took her up to the front porch. Warm light illuminated her, playing through her hair. Two sharp knocks and the door opened, revealing a couple.

Their smile was familiar. Returning their smile, Ava handed them the casserole. Their eyes lit up, and the woman hugged her.

After that, she returned to the car, and I set us in motion.

"What was that about?"

"What?" Her voice came out softer than earlier.

"The thing with the casserole?"

She folded her hands in her lap and looked out the window. "A few years ago, I started this...service when someone or a family is in need, I rally the folks in town to help."

"There are a bunch of locals, including Dad," she added with a chuckle, "who are committed to helping out and are on a rotation. When it's their turn, they cook something. Or if they don't want to cook, they do a grocery run for the family in need."

My heart squeezed. "You started this a few years ago?"

Ava's gaze whipped to me, her hair bouncing with her nod. "Yes."

I blinked, forcing myself to look back at the road. She'd been what? Eighteen? Twenty? How did a twenty-year-old think that up?

The charity dog wash picture flashed in my head. She'd always been that way. Always been kind and giving.

People like that were hard to come by. When I lived in the city, I met all kinds of people. People who did acts of selfless service were only a handful.

"That's amazing." My voice came out tight.

She shrugged. "I just do what I can."

I came to a stop outside her building.

"So."

"So," she returned slowly.

"Wanna invite me up for tea?" It was a joke. But...not really. I held my breath.

Ava's eyes pierced mine. Her mouth opened and closed. Chest rising and falling.

"I...we shouldn't."

"You really mean that?" I leaned forward, brushing aside the hair on her cheek.

Her body shivered under my touch. Her eyes fell shut. "Liam…"

I swallowed thickly. How could her sweet small voice be so damned sexy just saying my name? I ran a thumb over her lower lip.

"Ava?"

"We can't. It ends here." Her eyes popped open. "My Dad can never find out."

"He won't." My eyes latched onto her lips.

She moved closer and grabbed onto me, dragging my shoulders toward the center console. Our lips locked, and a collective sigh left us.

Her mouth moved against mine, almost painful in its desperation. Her hands twisted in my hair, pulling me deeper. I parted her lips and tasted her tongue.

"No." She yanked herself away, panting. "No."

Before I could speak, she hopped out of the truck and raced to the stairs that led up to her apartment. She disappeared. In the evening's quiet, I heard the click of a door.

I turned back, looking at the road, and sighed.

She would steer clear of me after tonight. For good reason. I needed to stop thinking with my dick.

It pulsed behind my zipper. Even after she was gone, the memory of her kiss was a sweet temptation.

But it was over, which was for the best.

Thomas could never find out. And I couldn't fuck her again.

I looked at Ava's lit-up apartment one last time, then set the car in motion.

Chapter 5

Ava

Dark gray clouds covered the sky, and a chill hung in the air. Still, the farmer's market bustled. The folks of Hannibal loved their Saturday shopping.

So did Linea and I.

The threat of a storm couldn't stop us.

We passed by stalls and booths. Stopped by some and looked through items, and haggled to no end.

"We can do this, you know?" Linea dropped a brush she'd been looking at.

"Do what?"

"Open a booth."

Linea was an enterprising woman. Every week, she came up with a new idea of something we could do.

I bit my lip. "I'm listening."

My friend spun on the spot. "Look around us."

Shoppers. Traders. A chilly, somber day.

"Yes?"

"Everyone comes out to shop on Saturdays, and we

don't work on Saturdays." She latched onto my arm, pinning me with hazel eyes. "We can start our own booth. Only open on Saturdays. We can sell cleaning products."

"Hmm, how's that different from the hundreds of products already on the market?"

"Come on." She dragged me to the next stall and picked up a bottle. "Look, just look at the ingredients." Linea read them out loud. "They're toxic. This is what folks use to clean their homes."

"Girl, if you don't drop my bleach…" The seller poked her head out of the stall.

Linea dropped it quickly, and we hurried along.

"Look, I'm not saying we'll make a fortune, but we stand a fair chance."

"It's a good idea," I mused. "Since most of what we use is organic, we can educate and enlighten others to use them, too."

"Exactly."

We split apart for a second to make way as a man passed with a heavy basket.

As we came back together, Linea added, "Plus, you know some people would like to use our services, but they can't afford it."

"Well, if we just—"

"No, Ava, we are not cutting back our rates."

I laughed. She knew me. We'd had this conversation lots of times.

Linea was sure if we didn't work together, I'd be cleaning homes for free.

She wasn't entirely wrong.

"Look, this would be a way to help them and still make money on the side. What do you think?"

"I—"

"Ava! Yoo-hoo, Ava."

I spun in the direction of the voice to see Mrs. Mullen. She was a stout woman in her forties. A few gray hairs played through her red hair. That hair now whipped around her face as she rushed to us.

"Hey, Mrs. Mullen." I smiled.

Linea offered a greeting, too.

"How are you today, girls?" She cast tender eyes between us. "Ava." She smiled warmly. "I can't thank you enough for the casserole."

My face heated. "It's nothing, and it was three weeks ago. Don't mention it."

"Well, the kids are still talking about it." She took my hand and patted it. "Thank you."

A smile curved my lips. "Dad made it. I just brought it over."

"Oh, Thomas. He sure does know his way around the kitchen. I hope I can return the favor someday."

I squeezed her hand. "I'm sure you'll get back on your feet in no time."

Sending one last smile between Linea and me, she said, "I sure do hope so. Have a lovely day, you two."

And then she was off.

"They do love you," Linea chirped.

"What? No." I continued through the aisles.

"You're very kind."

"Anyone would do that. Doesn't matter." To stop her from pressing the issue, I changed the subject. "So, about selling cleaning products."

"Mm-hmm." Linea perked up, compliments forgotten.

"What if we not only offered the products, but also a checklist?"

Her brows furrowed. "Like?"

"Well, we know houses get very cluttered over time, and the biggest reason they do so is the owners aren't keeping up daily. What if we create mock-ups of simple things they can attend to each day, so it doesn't pile up and overwhelm them?"

Linea stopped in her tracks.

I turned to her. "What?"

"God, Ava. I don't know what to do with you." She sighed.

"What?" I chuckled.

"Teach them how to organize their homes?" She gaped. "That's our whole thing — cleaning and tidying up out-of-control messy homes. If we showed them how, we'd lose business."

I thought for a moment. "Oh, I see."

"I'm glad you do." She shook her head. "I wonder how you'd make any money if I wasn't curbing your generosity."

"Linea!"

She giggled, walking ahead. "I'm just saying. You're like Santa Claus, but all year-round."

"Yeah, well," No argument popped up in my brain. "No one's complaining," I finished in a small voice.

"Aww, don't look that way." She turned, a smile in her eyes.

I shook my head. "You're impossible, Linea."

"The cleaning booth is still a good idea, though, right?"

I nodded. "Sounds fun. We could get a front stall."

"I think there's a charge. We can check, though."

"Yeah, we should—" My stomach swooped, heat rushing through my body.

I stopped on the path, trying to collect myself. Someone bumped into me and offered an apology. I couldn't speak.

Could only focus on standing as my head swam.

What was happening?

Warm hands touched my shoulder. "Ava, are you okay?"

I blinked at my friend. "I don't know. Just feeling dizzy."

She threw a gaze around, then pulled my arm. "Come with me."

Linea brought us to a sitting area and nudged me onto a chair.

"I'll be right back."

I buried my face in my hands and massaged my forehead. What's wrong with me?

"Here."

I pried my hands away. Linea held a can of soda before me.

"Thank you."

The first swallow washed down my throat, bringing some stability.

Linea dropped into the chair opposite me. "Feeling better?"

"A bit."

"What was that?"

I shook my head and drank deeply. "I have no idea. But…" I dropped the can on the table. "I've been feeling worn out lately."

Linea leaned in. "Since when? Why are you just telling me?"

"For about a week. It's nothing. Probably just been working too hard and burning myself out."

"Ava," she chided gently, "you do too much. What if you take Monday off and I cover for you? You can rest and—"

"What? No way." I sat up, and my head spun a little. I gritted my teeth against the sensation. "You can't do three houses all on your own in an eight-hour workday."

"But—"

"But nothing." I stood too fast but held my ground. "I'm fine." Somewhat. "I'll sleep in tomorrow, and I'll be fresh as a daisy by Monday."

Linea offered a reluctant, "Okay."

We resumed walking when she added, "But if you're the slightest bit dizzy again, you're going home."

"Agreed." Just to calm her down. I was fine.

We skirted the market's exit. "Did we get everything?"

Linea looked through her shopping bag. "We did."

That settled, we headed out. The open booths gave way to the town's streets, and soon, we walked toward my dad's grocery store.

"I'd like to say hi to Dad. I might not be able to make it for tomorrow's dinner."

"Cool," Linea said.

My stomach rolled, but I refused to mention it. I couldn't let her work alone on Monday.

To distract myself, I said the first thing that came to mind. Scratch that. The only thing on my mind.

"Did I tell you what Dad said about his friend?"

"Liam?" She grinned, eyes twinkling.

I had brought this upon myself.

"Yes."

"No, tell me." Linea scooted closer.

When I learned who he was, I told her that, but nothing more. She didn't push it, either.

Now, though, it'd been a week. Even though I thought about him daily, I could now speak of him without blushing to my toes.

And I was dying to tell Linea.

"Dad says he was a doctor in New York City. He got fed up with the rat race and decided to come to Hannibal for a quieter life."

"I would've sworn he worked with a secret service agency."

"Like a spy, right?"

"Yes, he has the look."

I chuckled. "He's just a doctor."

"A doctor you got down and dirty with." She pinched my side, wiggling her brows.

"Ugh, don't say it that way."

"But it was great sex."

"Linea!" I looked around, but no one paid us any mind. "Shh."

"What? You told me it's no big deal."

"Well, that was before I found out he's staying. He's setting up practice here."

"Oh, dear."

"Yep. So much for never seeing him again."

"Well..." Linea chewed on her lip. "I've got nothing. That's messed up."

My stomach churned. "It is."

"So, does your dad know?"

My heart leaped into my throat. "Of course not. And you won't say anything about it."

"I won't breathe a word of it."

We neared the grocery store, and I relaxed my shoulders. If I didn't tell my dad, and Linea didn't, then all would be fine.

Liam, too, had been cooperating, turning down my dad's dinner invites.

I was sure it was because of me.

I refused to let that make me feel any type of way. It was what I wanted.

Just then, my stomach clenched up, and a sick feeling heaved up my throat. I raced to the nearest trash can and bent over it.

My breakfast came up.

"Oh, dear." Linea appeared by my side, holding back my hair.

Another wave came, and I heaved again.

Linea muttered sorry over and over until my insides emptied. I sank on my heels, pulling in a deep breath.

"That was disgusting." I pushed aside the trash can.

My quip hung in the silence between us.

"Ava," she started, "how long have you been feeling rough?"

"A week." I ran a hand over my forehead. I had mentioned this before. "Why?"

Her eyes narrowed.

"What are you thinking?" I drew myself up, and a chill rushed through me.

"Well, when you slept with Liam, did you use—"

My stomach sank, and I shook my head. "No, it's not possible."

"Ava." She got up close in my face. "Did you?"

"We didn't, but—" I pressed a hand to my mouth, my lungs constricting. "It was only once. How's that possible?"

"Oh, no."

"Don't say that." My voice shook. "I'm not... I can't be..."

The word wouldn't leave my throat.

"Hey." Linea captured my shaking hands. "Look at me."

I stared into hazel eyes, forcing myself to remain calm.

"We don't know for sure. It's just a theory. Maybe you're at the height of your burnout." Her light tone rang hollow, and I couldn't muster a smile.

"Look, instead of speculating, what if I just got you a pregnancy test so we can be sure?"

I grabbed onto her arm and nodded toward my dad's store. "In there? What if Dad sees you? What if he asks?"

"He won't." She rubbed my upper arms. "Because you'll be distracting him."

I let out a sigh.

"Okay?"

"Okay."

"Ava?"

"I'm fine." I nodded, pulling in a breath. "Do what you need to do."

Linea headed into the store, and I came up behind her. My eyes went to my dad's office door. Bile rose up my throat.

I just might throw up again.

Chapter 6

Liam

I walked through the doors of my clinic, gazing around. Pleasure pooled in my stomach.

Just recently, the contractors had finished work on the space. I promptly had it scrubbed, top to bottom, and then stocked with medical supplies and equipment. Appointing staff was quick work, which brought us to now.

Liam Cooper's practice—open and receiving patients.

My clinic.

My throat clogged as I crossed the shiny floor. I should set up and get ready to meet patients. But I couldn't help pausing to take in the place.

Warm gray walls ran in a continuous sweep, only broken by renaissance-like nature paintings. Comfortable couches in a lighter shade of gray covered the space. A low brown coffee table adorned with a flower arrangement held magazines for patients.

The large windows tied it all together. They showed off the garden beyond, and light poured into the room.

All of it blended to form a peaceful, welcoming environment. That was what I needed for my patients.

Back in New York, I had no control over the hospital space where I worked. Everything was determined by management. Any changes they made racked up patients' bills.

It was disgusting.

But here, I could give proper care and not cut corners while doing so.

Not only did my patients have the best, but so did my staff.

I ensured the contractors paid attention to their workstations, outfitting them with good furniture and roomy space.

Judging by the warm greetings I received from the receptionist, the cashier, and the nurse, they loved it here.

We'd only started, but my gut said it was great so far.

The laboratory was through a door to the left, and I poked my head in. The lab scientist was by her post. I nodded a greeting and moved on.

The icing on the cake—the exam rooms—were spacious and bright. Just like the waiting room, I'd had the contractor make them warm and welcoming.

Even me, who wasn't a patient, felt like staying in the room.

Well, I would, since the first patients would be coming in soon.

I went to my office to do some paperwork before the day started.

Everything was different and unusual, but in a good way.

My chest bubbled over the more I thought about it.

I had transformed one side of my generational home into a clinic. Thank goodness for three generations of ancestors who'd bought massive plots of land. Even with the clinic, I still had the luxury of gardens and lawns.

All this wouldn't have been possible if I'd sold the property when my parents passed. I'd been tempted. There was nothing in Hannibal for me then.

But instead of selling, I rented it out.

Now I was grateful for my hesitation. Apparently, everything important to me was in Hannibal now.

My new life.

I pushed aside my work and swiveled around to stare out the window. The green, manicured lawn sent peace through my veins. Very different from the view of the city I had barely looked at before.

"Doctor," the nurse called from behind me. "The first patients are here. Should I send them in?"

And so it began.

The first person I saw was Mr. Harold. He came in with his daughter. Or rather, she dragged him in.

"He cut himself fixing the roof. He wanted to wash it out and call it a day."

"First," Mr. Harold protested, "I didn't cut myself fixing the roof. Don't say it like I broke my back. I was done fixing the roof, then on my way down the ladder, I cut myself."

"Same difference."

"It is different. You said I'd break my back. I didn't. Bringing me to a doctor in a...what is this place? It won't slow me down. I still have the patio to work on."

"It's a clinic, Daddy. And I'm only trying to take care of you."

I cut off Mr. Harold's grumble with a greeting. "You fix things a lot?"

"Yes. My home's my pride and joy, and I will not stop

just because I hit seventy." He threw a scathing look at his daughter.

"You look quite active for your age, and that's good."

A proud smile framed Mr. Harold's face. While I examined the cut on his arm, he told me about all the repairs he'd done on his home through last winter.

"I'll stitch this up so it heals nicely and give you some antibiotics to prevent an infection."

"Do what you have to, Doc." Mr. Harold looked a little less on edge.

I got that a lot at my former job. Older patients tended to be cranky. But there was never enough time to set them at ease.

It was rush, rush, rush.

All the damn time.

I hurried through examining patients like used syringes.

Now, though, after a session taking care of Mr. Harold's cut, he had calmed down. Even toward his daughter. They exchanged stories of funny doctor visits, even roping me into some.

"That'll be all for today," I told them, then gave a date for his next appointment.

Mr. Harold had zero issues with that. "I look forward to seeing you again, Doc."

Once they were gone, I could take the time to update his records before the next patient came in. Luxuries of a small-town practice.

Unlike Mr. Harold, the next patient was more reserved and quiet. I drew her out with a bit of conversation, and then she opened up and told me everything about her medical needs.

I responded appropriately, and when the session ended, she smiled at me.

"My family doctor was out of town, and I needed help. That's why I came here. I'm glad I did."

Damn. Way to melt my heart.

Patient after patient appreciated the services I offered. Some promised to recommend me to friends, and others made appointments for follow-up visits.

Pride grew in my chest. Of course, I wanted my patients to be well, but the truth couldn't be denied—people fell ill. I wanted Dr. Liam Cooper to be their preferred healthcare provider.

Lunchtime came around, and I settled into my office for a quick lunch. By choice, of course. At my former job, choice wasn't a luxury I possessed.

I was always on my feet. Always rushing from one exam room to the next.

Not that it wasn't important work. We did save lives, at least.

But *I* died a little each day.

I pushed away that unpleasantness and finished my meal. I did fulfilling work here, and it excited me to get back out there and see who needed my help next.

The nurse handed me a file. I cracked it open, reading through the vitals she took. The patient was in good health on paper.

Now to get to the bottom of their problem. I pushed open the door and stopped.

A woman sat on the exam table, legs folded at her ankles. Why did she seem familiar?

My gaze coasted up to the hands clenched in her lap, then higher, to a mane of rich brown hair pouring over her slender shoulders and covering her face.

Ava.

Even though I couldn't see her face, I had every other part of her body memorized, for some reason.

A reason I definitely wouldn't be exploring soon.

My heart thumped in my chest. She still hadn't looked up, but I hadn't closed the door yet, either. That would surely get her attention.

Why wasn't I doing that, though?

Because I was ogling her like a dolt. Shit.

I shut the door, determined to get myself together.

She jumped instead, her head whipping up, and her eyes met mine, widening. "Oh, God."

"No, just me. Liam." I smiled as I walked over.

But she didn't share my joke; she continued looking at me like I was a ghost.

"What—what are you doing here?" She blinked.

"Uh, I work here?"

Her gaze raked down my body, and my throat tightened. I was in scrubs—standard issue for my job description.

But her brown eyes flamed with something dark and suggestive, bringing me back to our first and only night together.

"No, you don't," she eventually supplied, meeting my eyes again.

I frowned. "What? Thomas didn't tell you?"

Her brows lifted, lower lip slipping between her teeth.

"Are you doubting me?" I reined in my laugh. "My name's on the door. Didn't you see?"

"No, I didn't. I was distracted. I—" Her eyes narrowed. "Wait here."

"I'm not going anywhere; I work here."

She tore past me, glaring as she passed.

I watched her disappear through the door. What the hell just happened?

Ava came back in the room after a few seconds. "You're...you're right. It is your practice."

I shook my head, unable to hide my smile. "Now that we've determined this is my clinic, can you tell me why you're here?"

Her face flamed, and she looked away. "No."

"No?"

"I—I can't." She hurried back to her purse on the exam table, snatching it up. "You can't help me."

What? "Ava, I'm a good doctor. Tell me your problem. We can get down to it."

"I don't have a problem."

I frowned. "You're at a clinic. No one walks in here unless they're having a health issue."

"Yeah, well, I just wanted to see how it looked on the inside. It's a new addition, after all."

"So you came sightseeing, then made an appointment? Really? You expect me to believe that?"

Her eyes flitted about before meeting mine. "Yeah, well. Yes."

"Huh."

"I'm thorough in my sightseeing."

When I said nothing, she spun in a circle, holding her arms out.

"I'm okay, see?"

I cracked open her file and read through it. Apart from taking her vitals, the nurse hadn't noted what she was in for. "Look, Ava. You don't have to worry." I shut the file and faced her. "What happened between us won't get in the way of me giving you the best care as your doctor."

Hell, it probably made me want to look out for her more. The urge I felt to care for her that first night we met surfaced again. I wanted to fix all her concerns, so she didn't look so pale and worried.

I left that part out, though. I didn't want to scare her off.

"You're safe here."

She took a step away from me. "I'm— I can't. You just have to promise me one thing."

My eyes narrowed, but I nodded.

"You won't tell my dad, alright? You won't tell him I was here."

"Why would I even—"

She closed the space between us, staring into my eyes. "Just promise me you won't tell him."

"Okay, okay. I won't." The worry in her brown eyes tightened my insides. "Look, even if you didn't ask, doctor-patient confidentiality would require I keep this visit private. No one outside these walls will hear of it. Is that what worries you? You can just sit down, and we'll—"

"I'm fine. That's all." She spun and rushed out of the exam room.

I peeked into the file again, like it held the answer. But there was nothing.

"Don't tell him."

I looked up. Ava had poked her head back into the room.

"Please."

"I promise."

Her face calmed somewhat, and she disappeared.

I doubted she'd be back.

As she so adamantly insisted, she was fine.

Hopefully, she really was and didn't need medical attention.

Or was she too embarrassed to let me attend to her?

Chapter 7

Ava

The sky above was a mix of burnt orange and reds with the sun's setting. Any other day, I'd be thrilled to stare in awe.

Now, I beelined for Linea's door and knocked, leaving the pretty sky behind.

"I'm coming," she grumbled.

Once the door cracked open, I pushed past her.

"Oh, Ava, come right in." She sidestepped out of the way. "Make yourself at home. Or whatever. It's not like I was falling asleep or anything important."

I ignored her sarcastic tone, shrugging off my jacket. The stupid thing caught on my hair. I wrestled with it, tangling myself even more.

"Um, Ava?" My friend drew close, her voice softer. "Are you okay?"

"I am not okay!" I spun on her.

Linea's eyes widened. "Oh, dear. Ava."

"I am not okay," I repeated, my body shaking.

"What happened at the doctor's? Is the baby alright?"

"I don't know." I let go of the jacket. It pulled at my hair, but I couldn't bring myself to care.

Everything was falling apart.

Linea drew closer and turned me, so my back faced her. "Let me get that for you while you tell me how it went."

I sighed. "It didn't go, Linea. The doctor didn't see me."

"I'm confused. Why not?"

"Well, he saw me, but—" She tugged at my hair. "Ow." I pressed a hand on the spot.

"Sorry. Your hair got tangled in a button. Tell me, what happened?"

The deep breath I took did nothing to calm me. "Linea, I feel like I'm in a freaking movie."

"A romance?"

"Romance? No! A freaking horror film."

"Wow. Was the doctor a monster?"

The jacket came loose, and I spun to face my friend. "Worse."

Her brows furrowed. "How?"

"It's Liam."

Her eyes widened, mouth agape. "You're kidding."

"I wish."

"But I don't understand. I thought you were going to Dr. Rogers."

"I was, but his clinic is closed for some reason, and someone told me there was a new clinic. I wasn't thinking. I was so distracted, I just walked in and spoke to the nurse. Only for me to find out it's Liam who's the doctor—after I was already in the exam room."

She covered her mouth, eyes anxious. "Does he know?"

53

My gaze fell. "No. I didn't tell the nurse why I was there."

"Oh, dear. This sounds—"

"Like a shitshow, I know." I closed my eyes, wishing I could erase the past day. I should have been more careful. Should have been paying attention.

"Do you think he suspects?"

"I don't know." I thought for a second. "He might, right? Some people can tell when someone's pregnant just by looking at them. What if he realizes? Or worse, tells my dad?"

"Calm down, Ava." Linea tossed the jacket on the couch and grabbed my arms. "Look at me."

Sympathetic hazel eyes held mine. "It's okay. We'll get through this."

"But how?" I broke away to pace around the space. "Not only is Liam my baby's father and my dad's best friend, but he also replaced the town's doctor. What am I to do? Who do I turn to?"

The pacing only amplified my worry, but I couldn't stop. "I'll be all alone. No one to help with the baby's delivery. What if something goes wrong? I can't do it, Linea."

I spun to my friend. "I can't go the natural route and do this by myself. Some women may be that strong. They never see a doctor through the pregnancy and push the baby out on all fours in their living room."

Linea's brow went up.

"Hell, they may even have someone playing drums and another standing with a delivery basket to catch the baby, but that is not my style. At all." My heart was racing, breath heaving from my lungs.

"Are you done?"

I planted my feet, my shoulders slumping. "Linea, I don't know what to do. I don't—"

"Hey, first, shh. You're not going to be pushing out your baby on all fours." She winced. "Thanks for the imagery, by the way."

"Lin…"

"Come on." She took my hand and lead me to the couch.

I plopped down, feeling the tension slip out of me slowly. But not completely. I still had the matter of…*every-thing* to figure out.

Jesus.

"Liam's not the only doctor in Hannibal. You can go see another one. Hannibal isn't that small."

"No, I can't." I scooted closer until our knees brushed. "What if word gets out?"

"Doctors have to keep their patients' details to themselves, Ava."

I gave her a look.

"But yeah, this is Hannibal. Somehow, shit always gets out."

"Yeah, and Dr. Rogers kept a tight lid on everything. I hoped a new doctor wouldn't be roped into the nonsense, but then the new doctor turns out to be Liam. The last person I want to see at the moment."

"Ah, your worry makes more sense now."

"And even if I wanted to brave it, what would I do if Dad finds out, or Liam?"

"But, Ava," Linea chewed on her lip, "Aren't you telling them at some point?"

"Well, yes." My heart rate sped up. Just the thought of it…how would I break it to them? I shut off the thought before I resumed pacing again.

"Not yet. Definitely not now." I carried on, "I need to know the baby's fine and healthy. I want to get a handle on things before bringing Dad and Liam into it.

But I don't want them hearing it secondhand from a gossip."

"Okay." Linea paused for a second. "I have an idea."

She left swiftly, returning with her laptop. "What if—" she popped it open and typed "—we find you a doctor in a town close by?"

The anxiety fisting my chest loosened. "That's a great idea."

"I know. I'm full of them."

I rolled my eyes and looked at the screen. "Not too close!"

"Fine." She canceled her search keywords and retyped. "What about three towns away?"

I calmed. "Yeah, that'll do."

We ran through five doctors and came to a woman with gentle eyes.

"Dr. Cynthia Morris," Linea read. "She looks nice. And her name is like yours. Morellis and Morris. She could be your aunt."

The deep blue eyes and rounded cheeks looked nothing like me. But her face didn't make me want to jump out of my skin.

"No, she couldn't. But I think I'm okay with her."

"Terrific. Let's book an appointment with Dr. Morris."

I released the breath I didn't realize I was holding. I leaned my head against Linea's shoulder. She paused typing to run a hand through my hair.

"It'll be all right."

Her quiet assurance warmed me. "I hope so."

DR. MORRIS WELCOMED me with a smile that deepened the lines around her eyes. She looked older in person, but no less kind.

"How are you, Ava? I'm Dr. Morris. Can you tell me what brought you in today?"

Dr. Morris took the news of my pregnancy smoothly.

Besides Linea, the doctor was the only person I'd told. I'd hyperventilated as my life flashed before my eyes. My friend, on the other hand, was thrilled.

She would be an aunt.

Now, narrating my situation to a person who accepted it so calmly settled my insides. Her eyes said everything would be all right. And it reassured me.

"Okay, Ava. You did the right thing coming to see me. I'll run some tests to ensure everything is fine with you and the baby."

I smiled, tearing up. "Thank you."

Her demeanor softened even more. "You're welcome." She flipped open my file and read. "What about the baby's father? Is he in the picture?"

"Not at the moment," I choked out.

She didn't miss a stride. "Anyone you can trust to support you?"

"Linea, my best friend." That may have come out too strong, but she'd been my rock this past week.

"Great friends are a treasure. It's good you have one. You may go to the lab for your tests now."

My results came in quickly, and I was called back to the exam room.

"Hi." I crossed the room to sit on the exam table, feeling at ease.

"Hi, Ava. I just got your results back from the lab."

I nodded.

"Everything checks out. The baby is great. You're fine, aside from one detail."

"You mean, minor detail?" I chuckled, nerves wrapping a cord around my belly.

Dr. Morris allowed a small smile. "Not so minor. Your blood pressure is a little high."

"It is?" My hand flew to my throat.

The doctor frowned. "Yes. I need you to manage your stress better. It's important for you and the baby."

I swallowed. "I understand."

"More sleep. More rest. Kick back and relax."

"Okay."

"If you're worried, talk to Linea. Or if it's medical, call the clinic, okay?"

I smiled. "Thank you, Doctor."

She returned my smile. "You're doing great, Ava. You'll be given some vitamins, and you should take them as recommended to boost your and your baby's health, okay?"

I nodded.

"Good. We're all done here."

The wind blew leaves across the streets on my drive back to Hannibal. For once, since I discovered I was pregnant, I felt at peace. Like I was headed in the right direction.

Even if the right direction was a couple of hours away from Hannibal and increased my gas bill. I was still okay.

The baby was fine. I was fine. I've got this.

A local station was on, and a pop song filled the car. I hummed along, not thinking of anything at all. I was content.

I came to a stop by the curb next to my apartment. A heavy sigh escaped me. It'd been a long week.

Thankfully, today moved things along positively.

I couldn't wait to take a nice warm bath, unwind, and just breathe. Finally. Everything would be alright.

I climbed the stairs up to my apartment. Just as I turned the corner, my eyes fell on a long, lean body propped against the wall. It straightened as I resumed climbing.

I crested the last step, and my eyes fell on Liam's. He was wearing a suit, the outfit complete with a silver watch. His hair was in place, impeccable as ever.

Despite his put-together look, something that tilted toward worry danced in his eyes. Did he know something?

Swallowing, I pushed forward. He couldn't. I went to a doctor three towns away.

"What are you doing here?" I sounded guarded, even to my own ears.

"I came to see you."

"That much is obvious. What do you want?"

He didn't flinch at my tone. If anything, a smile ghosted across his lips. "I've been thinking about you."

My heart leaped into my throat. The doctor had told me to relax and rest.

His warm, smoky voice, deep and seductive, didn't support rest. It demanded other things that'd speed my pulse up. Make my heart tremble.

A sizzling heat traveled up my thighs.

"Why—why are you thinking of me?"

"I've been worried since you ran out of my office the other day."

Oh.

"Are you alright?" he went on, stepping closer. His eyes traveled over my face and body.

My nerves prickled to life, wanting those eyes to be replaced by his hands.

I shook my head firmly. *No, Ava, don't go there.*

"You're not alright?" A frown deepened the lines on his face.

"No, no. I am. I'm just—" *Really hot for you.*

I gulped. "I'll tell you everything."

"Everything?" His brows lifted.

I nodded. There was no time better than the present, right? And now I knew the baby was fine.

Best to let the Liam know he'd soon be a daddy.

"Um, come on in. We can talk." I started around him toward the door.

His warm scent raced up my nostrils. My lungs expanded, wanting more.

I forced myself forward and inserted the key. By the time he learned everything, I was certain another round of hot sex would be the last thing on our minds.

"Alright."

My body shivered at the sound of his voice.

Yep, I needed to tell him ASAP, or I'd be throwing myself at him, begging for round two.

I pushed open the door, and Liam followed me inside.

Chapter 8

Liam

Ava drifted into the apartment, set aside her purse, and spun around. Her eyes were huge as saucers, lips trembling.

"Ava?" I stepped away from the door. "What's wrong?"

"I, uh." Her eyes met mine and then broke away. She swallowed. "Um, there's something I should tell you."

"I'm all ears."

"Okay." Her voice was small. She threaded her fingers, squeezing them. "So, remember the day I came to the clinic?"

I nodded, eager to get to the bottom of this. Whatever it was.

"Well…" She raised a hand and tucked a lock of rich brown hair behind her ear.

"Hey." Two strides brought me to her. I looked down into somber brown eyes.

My stomach twisted. I didn't come here to distress her. But it was all I seemed to do now.

Fuck.

"Come on, let's sit." I pried her left hand from the right and brought her to the couch.

We sat, knees touching, but Ava had retrieved her hand. She folded it in her lap now, playing with her fingers.

"So, can you tell me what's wrong?"

A heavy exhale left her body.

I waited. Whatever this was, it had to be significant. Or I wasn't the person she needed to speak to.

Why did the latter thought displease me so much? We weren't friends. We only slept together once.

Get it together, Cooper.

"Ava?"

"I-I'm trying." She sighed.

"I'm here for however long it takes."

Her eyes coasted back up to mine. The freckles across her face stood in sharp relief. Her nose quirked in a question.

"I'm not leaving you." I took her hand. "Whenever you can, let it out."

She curved her small hand into mine, drifting closer. "Thank you, Liam."

I squeezed her hand.

"You're not so bad when we're not at my dad's, and you're not trying to make me mad."

I chuckled. "You should have seen your face."

"I panicked!" She sat up. "Didn't you?"

I shrugged. "I know you won't tell him. Neither will I. So it's all good."

Her shoulders fell again, and she sighed. "I wish I were as confident as you."

"Are you still worried about your dad finding out?"

"No, not exactly."

"Then what?"

She didn't respond and wouldn't look up.

I reached across the space and brushed away the hair from her cheek. Just to see her face. Figure out what was going on in her head.

My fingers grazed her soft skin, and awareness rushed through me. Then my thumb moved, stroking gently.

I couldn't stop if I tried. Didn't want to.

Her eyes met mine now, like she felt the same. She shut her eyes for one long minute and pushed her face into my palm.

I swallowed thickly and moved forward. Our legs intertwined. I palmed her face and continued rubbing her cheek with my thumb.

Her head fell to the side, exposing a long, slender neck. My fingers followed, tracing a path down, making her skin blush a pretty pink.

She sighed shakily before looking at me again. "You calm me," she whispered.

"I do?" I played with the ends of her hair, settling them around her shoulders.

"Mm-hmm." She nodded.

"I'm glad I can help."

Silence followed. Yet, not completely.

My heartbeat thudded, and Ava's breath came out in pants.

She broke the spell, leaning into me.

Her soft body sent an eager shiver down my spine. I clutched the curve of her hips, and my cock thickened in my dress pants.

"Do you want to help me some more?" she asked breathlessly.

"How?" I croaked. I couldn't refuse her anything.

Not now, not when she looked at me like I held the world in my hands.

Her eyelids drooped, her head tilting.

I drifted close and pressed my lips to hers.

Ava's reaction was instant. Her body sagged against mine.

A groan escaped. I traced my hand back to her nape, tilting her head just right so I could better devour her lips.

But she pulled away, gasping.

I half expected her to scramble away. But she only stared at my face with pure adoration.

"Your kisses make me feel better."

"Ava," I breathed, my voice unsteady. "You shouldn't say stuff like that."

"Why not?" Her lips pursed, then softened. "That's how I feel."

"I know, but…"

The last thing I wanted to remind her of was her dad. It'd surely break the spell of the moment. But we shouldn't be doing this.

Still, I wanted her more than anything else right now. And one more night together wouldn't hurt, right?

I worked my hands down her body. Rubbed my palms along the soft swell of her breasts. I ran my thumbs over her nipples and felt them stiffen through her top.

Her whimper turned my blood to lust.

I shouldn't be doing this.

I skimmed the edge of her panties, and her breath sucked in.

"Touch me, Liam," she whispered, trembling against me.

Before I could form a reply, she began planting kisses on my neck.

Sweet fuck. "Ava." My body shook with restraint. "We shouldn't."

"I can't help it." She sucked on my neck, then licked her way to my earlobe. "I need you."

My fingers dug into her hips, and my breath turned heavy in my chest. Her pants bathed my neck with heat.

She needs me.

How could I say no?

"All right, Ava, I'll take care of you."

She sat back, staring at me. Her tongue snaked out and traced her lower lip. "H-how?"

I let my gaze drift down, then up her body. Our eyes met. "Lie down. On your back."

Ava obeyed quickly. She lay down, and her hair fanned about her face. Her chest rose and fell rapidly, pushing her tits up at her neckline.

But that wasn't what pulled a groan from my throat.

She pulled her skirt up, bunching her dress around her waist, revealing white lacy panties.

I'd seen her naked before. But the damp spot at the apex of her thighs hardened my cock. Made me throb with want.

The need to plunge into her wet heat and possess her.

I knelt before her and kissed both knees. "Be a good girl and open up for me, Ava."

Her body trembled, eyes glazing over.

She liked when I called her a good girl.

I see.

She always helped people. Caring, responsible Ava. And she wanted her reward in kisses.

My cock pulsed. I was good at giving attention and care.

I rubbed her outer thighs, coaxing her. "Open up, sweetness."

Her legs came apart a little, and my eyes feasted on her creamy thighs and her wet core.

"Want to make me work for it?" My voice dropped to a low growl.

She made me wild; I couldn't help it.

Her mewl was a fist around my cock.

I dove in, kissing and licking her inner thighs. Her legs parted some, bringing me closer to her heat.

I sniffed her arousal, pushing my nose into her folds, then licked the wet patch. Her cry begged for more.

Too willing to oblige, I fingered aside her panties and pressed my tongue into her heat.

She tasted sweet and musky, just how I liked it.

My eyes fell shut, my whole being attuned to hers. She bucked into my face, fingers gripping my hair.

She shoved me deeper, moving her hips to the rhythm of my licking.

"Yes!" Her hips shook, losing their rhythm.

I grabbed her hips, holding her down and circling her swollen clit. "Do you like this?" I sucked her into my mouth. "Like how I take care of you, Ava?"

"Yes, yes!" she cried. "Right there, don't stop!"

I kept up the steady pace, letting her grind onto my face.

"Oh, God. I'm going to—oh, yes, daddy!"

I froze.

A shocked gasp followed, but Ava's lower body still flexed, the orgasm hitting her hard.

"Liam, oh, I meant—" She sucked in a feverish breath. "What I meant was…"

Her center still pulsed around my tongue.

"I didn't mean it that way." She collapsed with a sigh.

Her juices were wet on my lips, and I withdrew to savor them.

Ava's eyes were on me. Wide and worried. "Liam, are you mad?"

I kissed her folds, and she whimpered. "Do you want me to be?"

"I don't know where that came from. That's all. I don't want you to be mad," she ended in a small voice.

I kissed her thigh and sat back on my haunches. "Take off the dress. Everything."

Ava got off the couch, her knees shaky. She undid the zipper and pulled off the dress. Then her bra and her drenched panties dropped to the floor.

I stroked myself twice to the view of her supple body.

"Get back on the couch. The way you were before," I rasped.

She hesitated, tangling her hands before her, shielding her pussy.

"Now, Ava."

"You sound angry."

I stood, rounding on her. She took a step back, but I snatched her by the waist and drew her flush against me.

She gasped.

"Feel that?" I rocked against her stomach.

My cock turned to steel.

I kissed the shell of her ear. "Feel how hard I am?"

She nodded.

"That's the only thing that makes me mad, Ava. That I'm not inside your sweet little pussy yet."

"Liam."

"No, the other name."

"Liam, I don't think—"

I pinched her chin and brought her face up. Her wide brown eyes stared back at mine.

"I know you want to. Do it."

Her lips parted. "D-"

I circled my hips. "Do you want my cock? Want daddy's cock?"

She whimpered, trembling.

"Be a good girl, Ava." My voice came out rough. "Say you want daddy's cock."

"I want your cock—" *swallow* "—daddy."

"Now, was that so hard?" I kissed her lips.

She opened up for me, letting me taste her tongue, and likely tasting herself on my lips. I pulled away just as she turned breathless. Heavy-lidded eyes blinked at me.

"Go get it, Ava. Play with daddy's cock."

She kissed down my body, drawing a hiss from my mouth. Her hands made quick work of my belt buckle and zipper. My pants pooled around my legs, followed by my boxer briefs.

Seeing Ava poised to lick my shaft sent my hips slamming forward. The tip brushed her lips, and she opened up.

Her hot little mouth closed around me, and I groaned.

"Ava." I fisted her hair and thrust.

She moaned and pinched her nipple with one hand. The other wrapped around the base of my cock, urging me deeper.

Pleasure tingled down my spine, making me want to thrust hard until I came. But I wanted her in another way.

I yanked her up and spun her around. "I'm in need, Ava. Want to make me feel good?"

"Y-yes. Oh, yes." She rubbed her ass on my cock.

I groaned as precum spread across her pert cheeks.

"Good girl, Ava. Now lean forward."

She placed both hands on the backrest of the couch, knees planted on the cushion. Her core lined up with my cock, and I thrust.

Just the tip slipped in.

"Fuck." The sight of it. Her dripping wet hole trying to swallow me.

I leaned forward so my chest was to her back, and sank in deep.

We cried out at the same time.

"God, Ava. You're so tight." I drew a ragged breath. "I'm not going to last."

"Don't stop, daddy," she whined. "I want your cum. Now."

Fuck. My body jackknifed, pounding in and out of her.

I held her hip to steady her. Wrapped an arm around her body to play with her bouncing tits.

She moaned loudly, spreading her legs and curving her spine. My cock sank deeper.

Pleasure blinded me.

"Ava, oh fuck!"

She captured the hand on her hip and put my fingers on her clit.

I teased her as my pace picked up so fast I was hammering into her wildly. Pulling almost the whole way out, and thrusting back in. Reaching for our ecstasy.

"Oh, I'm going to come!" Ava fell back against me, rocking her hips. "I'm coming, daddy."

The last word, her clenching depths, her whimpering cry. All of it forced my orgasm.

It hit so hard I collapsed with her onto the chair. I sucked her neck hard as I continued to fuck her pussy in punctuated motions.

"Look how you drive me crazy, Ava." I breathed against her neck. "Look how... Fuck." I drove my cock inside her as she took the last of my cum. "Does this make you feel good? Feeling better?"

"Yes. Yes, daddy."

Pleasure that had nothing to do with fucking sliced through me.

Why did this feel like a beginning, and not an end?

Chapter 9

Ava

Damn it, I did it again. I slept with Liam Cooper.

My body sizzled with the memory of his hands, mouth, and his deep voice saying that forbidden name.

I shut my eyes and let the memory wash through me.

Daddy. Come play with daddy's cock.

Who knew I liked kinky talk like that?

I certainly didn't realize.

But when Liam kissed me, touched me, and said he'd take care of me, the dam broke. The literal dam on all my fantasies.

He took charge. He made me forget with the kisses he landed everywhere.

I was nearly breathless.

Unfortunately, last night had to end and bring on another work day. Instead of spending time kissing Liam and having him possess me again, I was busy cleaning. Elbows deep in scrubbing a grimy sink.

My gaze drifted out the window to the mowed lawn.

If I could rewind time and do it all over again, I would. Ten times over. And maybe spend the whole day savoring his cock a little longer.

"Ava!"

I jumped and spun around. "What?"

Linea eyed me. "Where did your mind go?"

"Nowhere."

"You were staring out the window, your hands frozen. Is there something interesting out there?"

Linea came over to the sink and peeped out. "Not that I can see. So what's with you?"

"What?" I drew in a discreet breath and returned to cleaning the sink.

"Something is up. What aren't you telling me?"

I side-eyed my friend. "Seriously? I was only thinking of our schedule for the coming days. We have a lot of work to do."

"So, schedules make you blush?" She put her messy finger on my face.

"Hey!" I batted her hand off. "That's nasty."

"Doing the nasty is what you were thinking about." Linea didn't budge.

My stomach fisted. Did she know? No, she couldn't.

"Can we just get back to work?" I affected a bored tone.

Linea saw right through my act. "Uh-uh," she declared. "Tell me."

"There's nothing to tell."

"You're practically glowing today. Humming to yourself. Staring out the window."

"I was looking at the new plants."

"You said you were thinking of our schedule."

My face heated. "I—"

"You are *so* lying to me. There's something you're not telling me."

"Linea, we have so much work to do today."

"So you better start really quick. You don't want to disappoint our clients by being a secret-keeping..." She chewed her lip. "Keeper of secrets."

My brows knotted. "That's essentially the same thing."

"I don't care. Just tell me now." She chuckled. "What has you in such a state? Did the doctor say you're having triplets or something?"

"Oh, God, no." My hands went to my stomach. "Don't even think that!"

"It could happen." Linea nodded.

I curled my hands around my stomach. "Linea, stop. You're scaring me."

"Then give up your secret, or I'll describe the other possibilities—"

I pressed my hands against my ears and yelled, "I slept with Liam."

Silence filled the kitchen following my confession.

I pried open my eyes to see Linea staring at me.

"Do you mean like, the first time, or..."

The truth was already out there. No use lying. "Last night."

"Ava." Her eyes bulged and she smacked my shoulder.

"Ow." I stepped back and hit the counter. "What's that for?"

"How could you sleep with him again?" Linea's voice dropped into a whisper.

No one could hear us since the family was either at school or work. But the hushed sound made everything more ominous.

"Well..."

"You're digging a hole it'll be hard to climb out of, Ava." She drew close till I could see the brown flecks playing in her eyes. "What do you think is going to happen?"

She plodded on. "You'll fall for him, and everything will blow up in your face."

"But—"

"No buts. The first time, you didn't plan for it. But this?" Her shoulders fell. "You need to make better decisions, Ava. Get ahold of yourself."

"But," I raised a finger. Linea eyed me. "It's a good 'but!'"

"Fine, what's the reason?"

"The sex is just so amazing," I gushed.

"Oh, for heaven's sake, Ava." Linea facepalmed. "What am I going to do with you?"

I skirted around her, continuing my cleaning. "First, don't be so judgy. Second, wipe that look off your face."

"But I'm worried about—"

I raised the hose and squirted her face.

Her frown turned to shock. "What was that for?"

"Washing your frown off." I grinned. "Did it work?"

"Oh, let me see. I think—" Linea wrestled the hose out of my hands and sprayed my shirt.

I screamed, skirting out of the way. But the small kitchen didn't leave much room for escape. I went on the offensive, collecting the hose and returning the favor.

"Stop, stop!" Linea raised both hands. I give up."

Laughing, I dropped the hose. "Good."

"Ugh, now we need to clean the floors."

I looked down and shrugged. "We were going to do it anyway."

"Yeah, yeah." Linea retook her spot by the stove.

We were soaked. The floor beneath our feet needed

extra cleaning, but the air was clear. No untold secrets clogged up my brain, and I could think.

We finished the cleaning in record time. Done with that, we loaded all our cleaning tools and products in my car's trunk.

The next house was across town, but thankfully, the traffic was moving along. We arrived in record time.

It was another empty house, save for a house cat. Linea grabbed the little gray fur ball the moment we walked through the door.

"Hey, you. Have you been a good girl, huh?" She went upstairs with the cat.

While she was busy with the family's pet, I unloaded the trunk.

She came back down without the cat. "What have we got?"

"Messy living room," I announced.

Linea crossed the space and peeked into the kitchen. "Untidy in there, too."

"We better get cleaning."

While I removed the cobwebs, Linea was in charge of dusting furniture and vacuuming.

Fifteen minutes later, I paused and wiped my brow. "Look at it this way—"

"If you're about to tell me the details of your sex life, don't."

"Oh, you know what? Maybe I will. He put his hands on my hips and…"

Linea pressed her hands to her ears and sang "la, la, la," over and over.

I hollered my made-up sex story, and she groaned.

"Make it stop!"

Chuckling, I said, "Fine, I'll stop. Promise."

"Okay." She pulled her hands away. "What were you going to say?"

I bit my lip. "Should I tell Dad about the pregnancy? He'll be surprised, no doubt. But after that, I'm certain he'll be supportive and will help me figure out what to do."

I dropped the duster and put a hand to my flat stomach. "I've been thinking a lot, and I know in my soul I can't part with my baby, ever."

My eyes met Linea's. "For months, I've wanted an adventure. What if this is it?"

Her lip quirked in a small smile. "I think telling your dad is a good idea. Come on, he's always been there for you. Even when you're being an absolute nightmare, drama queen, screeching mess—"

"Hey!"

She chuckled. "He cares for you a lot, Ava. And after the initial shock, he'll be thrilled to be a grandpa."

My insides warmed. "You think so?"

She nodded.

I exhaled and closed my eyes.

I could almost picture my dad grinning at his grandson or granddaughter. Fussing over them. Giving his signature head rubs to them.

Yes, I loved this turn of events.

"But," Linea's voice yanked me back to the present. "All his joy might go out the window when he finds out who's the father."

My heart plunged into my stomach. "Oh crap, that's true."

I paced around the room. "That's the problem, right? If I tell my dad, he'll tell Liam, and it'll come out somehow that Liam's the father."

"So, what if you told Liam first, and he keeps it to

himself? Then when your dad finds out, it'll be no news to Liam."

I swallowed a breath. "That's not what I'm afraid of."

Linea frowned. "What, then?"

"If I tell Liam I'm having his baby, I doubt he'll just say 'okay' and walk away."

"Do you want him to?"

"Well, no. I just—" I clenched my teeth. It must sound selfish, but I knew and trusted my gut. Aside from the fantastic sex and Liam being my dad's friend, he was a stranger.

"If he gets involved, it wouldn't just be what I want for the baby. He'll bring his ideas, and I don't know if we'll even agree."

"Oh, dear." Linea crossed the room and hugged me.

I breathed in the mild scent of our organic cleaning products. The cord around my chest loosened a bit. Even if my life was turning on its head, I could trust some things to remain the same.

Like the warmth of Linea's hug, her support, and her kindness.

"Hey." She pulled away and took my hands. "Whatever happens, you've got this, okay?"

I frowned. "I don't want *whatever* to happen. Why can't it all just be easy?"

"Life's not that way. So put on your big girl panties. You'll get through this."

I smiled, despite the worry churning through me. "Thank you, Lin. You're the best."

"I know." She returned to her post.

While Linea resumed dusting, I faced my tasks with a new determination. Anything to distract me from my thoughts.

But nothing worked.

By the time we finished, my body ached, seeking rest. My frayed mind came to its own conclusion.

I needed to tell Liam.

He was the father and he should know. Whatever he decided to do with the information was his choice. But I owed us that much.

Yet, jumping right in with such an announcement didn't sit right. If he was a boyfriend I'd dated for a while, it'd be a no-brainer.

I'd only seen Liam three times, and two of those times, we hadn't done much talking. The night we had dinner at my dad's could've been spent getting to know each other better. But I was too mortified by the discovery that he was my dad's friend.

Liam was great in the sack, but that didn't necessarily make him a good man. Or a good father, when the time came. I had to get to know him first before inviting him into my baby's life.

I needed to spend more time with him. Find out if we were compatible.

We could...date.

A tremor swirled through me. Thinking about sitting across a table from Liam, having his storm gray eyes focused on me, tickled something in my stomach.

Was that attraction or something more?

God, my insides were a mess. I needed to give it time.

Give us time.

If we weren't compatible in the romantic sense, at least I'd find out if he'd make a decent co-parent.

Get to know him. That's what I'll do.

Chapter 10

Liam

I closed the office doors shortly after five o'clock. It was still strange to be done with work so early. Back in NYC, I'd still have another four hours before finishing my shift.

Here, life was much more relaxed. I was back at my house before dark, peeling off my scrubs on the way to the bedroom.

Today was a long day by Hannibal's standards. I saw many patients and was on my feet most of the time. But in the end, it was short compared to the hours I pulled in the city at the hospital.

I wasn't used to feeling so fulfilled, yet without the exhaustion that had become my norm. My blood still pumped with energy.

I thought I was old, and that's why I couldn't keep up in the city. Turns out, I was just overworked.

Spending the evening leisurely seemed like a viable option, but inactivity bored me. I needed to do something. Like going out and meeting people.

A particular brown-eyed, freckle-faced brunette popped into my head. Would she be at Busters? The last time we saw each other there was a Friday, and today was a Wednesday.

Or I could go to her house again.

I cringed. That'd be coming on too strong. Plus, the matter of her dad still hung over us.

I tore my eyes away from my button-downs and grabbed a T-shirt. The best option was to stay at home and avoid the temptation to seek out Ava.

Thank goodness, I had something to keep me busy. I planned to install a new deck on the back of the house. No better time than to start than now.

I pulled on some sweatpants and headed downstairs. I searched the fridge for a beer, cracked it open, and headed out back.

The sun was setting and poured golden light over the space. I sucked in the cool, crisp evening air and exhaled.

I'd start working in a moment, but first, I took a few minutes to enjoy Hannibal's quiet.

Only a few weeks here, and it already felt like home. Work days were long, but granted the peace I'd needed. It aligned with what I'd desired for a long time.

The people were also kinder. Life was much more straightforward. Everything was more colorful and beautiful.

And I was turning into a sentimental man.

I took another swig of my beer before setting it on a table.

While the backyard stretched out, ending at a fence, the patio was short. It limited the outdoor living space. To remedy that, I had purchased fine, sturdy wood.

I'd add a new deck and maybe a firepit. With the

image fresh in my head, I grabbed a measuring tape and the length of wood I'd need.

I measured and marked the lumber, then grabbed a saw and started cutting.

My breath heaved, sweat gluing my shirt to my back, but it felt good. I was used to working in an office with no break for physical activities. Today, I welcomed the tightness in my upper arms and abdomen.

Something new for a change.

A doorbell chimed.

I paused, frowning. Was it coming from a neighbor's house? I doubted it.

Empty land stretched in both directions around my home. It wasn't possible to hear a thing from the next house.

It rang again.

Someone was at my door. That set me in motion.

My brows pinched. Could it be a medical emergency?

In the days since I'd returned, no one had ever come to my home after work.

I pulled open the front door. "Ava?"

She smiled, her cheeks turning pink. "That's me."

My heart pumped faster. "Um, come on in."

"Thanks." Her smile still in place, she walked into my home.

I drank in her fresh fragrance and stifled a groan. So sweet. Somehow, my voice stayed even despite my senses going into overdrive. "How are you?"

She turned to face me. "Come on, I know you're dying to know why I'm here."

I chuckled lightly. "Well, yeah. That, too."

"I brought takeout." She lifted a bag. "Hungry?"

That was a no-brainer. "Starving. I was working out back. Wanna join me?" I headed toward the kitchen.

"Sure." She trailed behind me.

The sun was falling swiftly in the sky, but there was enough light still.

I made my way to the old table and chairs and grimaced. They looked alright when I was alone. Now they seemed dingy next to Ava, dressed in her flowery dress and sandals.

"We could go back inside."

She shook her head. "I love it out here."

To make her point, she dropped into one of the chairs. It creaked, but as she settled in, it quieted.

I took the chair opposite.

She unpacked the bag and handed me a box with a fork, taking the other one for herself.

We opened both boxes, and the aroma of chicken chow mein filled the air.

"Nice," I murmured, then dug in.

"I know," she moaned. "So delicious."

I studied her face in the waning light. Suddenly, I was more interested in the warm glow of her skin than the best chicken chow mein I'd had in a long time.

A cool breeze was ruffling her hair, lifting the strands before they settled again on her shoulders. If I could make a wish, it'd be to have the right to caress her skin the same way.

Ava stopped mid-chew. "What?"

"You really came just to bring me dinner?"

Her throat bobbed. "No, not just that."

I sat up, interested. Maybe she'd finally tell me what had her so worried the other day.

"I'd like to get to know you."

I paused, my eyebrow lifting. "Is that so?"

She bit her lip, then nodded. "Yes."

"Huh." I brought a helping of noodles into my mouth, chewed, and swallowed. "What would you like to know?"

"Well, why did you come to Hannibal? No offense, I love my hometown, but compared to New York, this is backwoods as backwoods can be."

"Really? You think that? New York is a dense hub. Everyone is always rushing and hustling from one place to the next. I like how laid-back and quiet Hannibal is."

Her eyes watched me carefully, hanging onto every word. Usually, people were telling me about their ailments and problems. But seeing her interested in what I had to say, genuinely interested, kept me talking.

"The air is clean here. People here are nice."

"Like me?" She teased.

A laugh worked up my throat. "Yeah, of course."

Her giggle carried on the wind. "That may be one of the reasons I like Hannibal, too."

"Because you're nice?"

"What? No." She laughed.

I felt my lips stretch in a smile. "But you just said—"

"Stop." She pointed her fork at me, still trembling with laughter. "I meant I like Hannibal because of the ambiance and the people. They're great. It's a nice place to live."

I thought back to the picture of her during the charity dog wash. She was one of those great people of Hannibal. If I brought it up, I had no doubt she'd downplay it.

Instead, I asked, "So you've never thought of leaving?"

She looked up at the darkening sky, like it held all the answers. "Well, I did once. But it was only a passing thought. I was mad at my dad, and I told him the moment I turned eighteen, I was leaving."

"What?"

"Yeah, I kinda wasn't the most pleasant teenager."

I pictured a younger Ava fuming with rage.

"What? Why are you smiling?" She eyed me.

"You must have been adorable, declaring your quest for freedom."

Her cheeks flamed. "I wasn't adorable. I was mad at my dad."

"Why?"

"He tossed out my favorite boy band poster."

My eyes narrowed.

"That's all?"

"I was a teenager!"

I chuckled. "You're so adorable when you're mad."

"Ugh, and you're annoying." But a reluctant smile covered her face. "It's no laughing matter."

"I know." I pressed my lips together, barely containing my laughter. "Serious, life-changing stuff."

She sighed. "Yeah, well, I never left. As you can see."

She shrugged. "I love being here. My life is here. Everything I care about. All the people I love. It's home."

"It's starting to feel like home for me, too." My voice came out gruffer than I expected.

Ava's eyes softened and her fingers twitched. Like she wanted to reach across the table and take my hand in hers.

Warmth filled my chest. Why did I want that?

"So, where did you get this chow mein? I could eat it all day." I faced my meal and took another bite.

If Ava noticed I was deflecting, she ignored it and gave me the restaurant's name.

We ate in silence for a few moments before she piped up again.

"So, about you and Dad, what was your friendship like before you left? How long have you known each other?"

The memories brought a smile to my face. I set aside the almost empty container and leaned back.

"Your dad and I became friends in elementary school. Can't remember how exactly, but we just clicked over something. That was a lifetime ago."

She smiled.

"Anyway, Thomas was always bigger than me." I raised both arms, imitating his bulky build.

Ava laughed. "I can imagine that."

My lips twitched. "Well, I eventually filled out. I didn't stay a scrawny kid forever."

Her eyes roamed over me, as if trying to confirm. "Well…"

"What?"

"No, oh my gosh." She pressed her hands to her face. "I'm just saying… Dad has always been larger than life and I've seen his childhood pictures, so I get it."

"Hmm." I kept my gaze on her, enjoying her deep blush. "You're off the hook. For now."

"Ugh." She rolled her eyes, humor dancing in their depths. "Just tell me more."

"Since your dad was bigger and more assertive than me, he turned into something of a protector. When I got bullied, he was there to defend me. When we became teens, no one messed with either of us because Thomas was so strong."

"Aww." Ava stared at me with compassion. "Dad's like a big teddy bear now. Can't picture him being all threatening."

I chuckled. "He was threatening, alright. I eventually grew into my frame—" I gave her a pointed look "—and we joined the football team."

I reclined, thinking back to the simplicity of those days. "We had all our firsts together."

"Uh, excuse me?"

I shot up straight. "Like playing sports, first jobs, and sharing dreams of leaving Hannibal!"

"Oh, okay." Ava grinned. A frown stole across her face. "Wait, you said leaving Hannibal. Why did you leave, but not my dad?"

I chuckled. "He met a girl, fell in love, and had you."

Her eyes warmed. "My mom?"

I nodded. "She was about your age. Very excited to be a mother. Your dad was scared shitless, though."

"Sounds like Dad." She laughed. "But he came around to the idea of fatherhood?"

Her eyes were strangely solemn.

"Yes, he loves you very much. I don't think he'd have changed a thing."

She smiled gently. "Okay."

I wanted to round the table and pull her into my arms, maybe kiss her to emphasize my sincerity. But something about just sitting and talking with her felt so much more meaningful.

The sky was dark now, the backyard only lit up by the outdoor lighting. The warm glow played across Ava's expressive features as she asked me more about my life.

I settled in, my heart filling with contentment. This felt...right.

Chapter 11

Ava

Hours must have passed since I arrived at Liam's house.

It was dark outside and the air was much cooler. Yet, it felt like mere minutes since I climbed the porch steps and rang the doorbell.

The outdoor lighting behind me danced in his eyes, giving them an otherworldly quality. He leaned back in his chair, a stealthy strength in his arms and chest.

Something twisted in my belly.

What if I crawled over the table and climbed into his lap? Would he wrap his arms around me? Call me a *good girl* again?

A thrill feathered across my neck and I shivered. *I wish.*

"Are you getting cold?" Liam sat up.

"No, I'm fine."

"It is chilly." He looked around. "And dark. I've kept you out here for too long."

Not long enough. I almost said the thought out loud.

He drew up to his full height and started clearing the table.

He claimed my dad used to be much bigger than him. If that was right, he'd filled out quite nicely.

I licked my lips, wondering what it'd feel like to run my tongue down his body. Maybe pull his cock into my mouth. Let him thrust deep into my throat.

Another shiver rocked my body.

Liam missed nothing. His eyes turned to slits, jaw clenched. Like he was mad.

"Let's go inside." He drew me up by the arm. "Quickly."

I laughed, rising to my feet. I'd been doing that—laughing—a lot tonight.

Laughing. It was so easy with Liam.

Most of the time, he was so serious. The only emotions I could detect from him were hiding in his eyes. Yet, the atmosphere around him was warm and welcoming.

Maybe that was what made him such a good doctor. My insides seized up. I wanted to be the only being taken care of by him.

It made me want to throw myself into his arms and stay there forever.

We crossed the threshold into the house. Liam let my hand go and headed to the trash can. I clenched my fist, missing his warmth.

Once he disposed of the empty takeout containers, he made his way to the sink. His face was set in a firm line as he washed his hands, giving attention to every inch.

I couldn't help myself. "What are you doing?"

He turned, cocking his head. "Washing my hands?"

The overhead bulb was softer than the light outside and made his face kinder.

"I know. But you're scrubbing every finger. So thorough."

"Come on." He waved a soapy hand.

I hesitantly moved closer.

"Give me your hands." He reached out with his own.

I eyed them, then placed mine in his.

One side of his mouth ticked up. Using my hands, he drew me close.

"Hands under the faucet."

I swallowed and did as he asked. He moved from my side for a second. The very next, his body was covering mine from behind.

I sucked in a breath, feeling everything. His chest against my back, his palms covering the backs of my hands, his breath on my neck.

"Let's wash, shall we?"

Did he just nudge my nape with his nose?

Before I could make sense of that, a sweet feeling traveled from my fingers up my arms. Liam was washing my hands.

No, washing wasn't quite right.

He took each finger, caressing it softly, massaging the soap into it. His thumbs rubbed my palms gently, up to my wrists, then back down.

My breath stuck in my lungs. My heartbeat slowed.

I couldn't do anything. Just feel.

My eyes fell shut and I savored his closeness.

"How does this feel?" he whispered against my neck.

"Um." I licked my lips. "Good."

"Thoroughly cleaned hands are good," he said, a hint of humor in his tone.

I blinked open to see him looking at my face over my shoulder. Not just at me.

His eyes took in all my features. From the freckles

across my nose to my eyelashes. They came to rest on my lips.

I felt them part.

The rush of cold water snapped me out of my trance. I focused on my hands as Liam rinsed them off.

"There you go." His voice still had its hypnotic quality. "All clean."

I pulled my hands back and skirted away from him, finally managing to pull a deep breath. "Yep, feels good."

He chuckled, snatched a towel, and tossed it at me.

I caught it quickly and wiped my hands. Just to have something to do other than ogling him, I looked around the house.

It had high ceilings with wooden beams running across them. The walls were covered in a warm beige color and beneath my feet was lovely hardwood flooring.

I'd always thought it was one of the most beautiful old homes in town when I drove past. But now, being inside was even more fascinating.

"Your home is beautiful," I blurted out.

"It is."

I turned to Liam but he wasn't looking at the space around us. His eyes were zeroed in on me, dark and intense. I lost my train of thought.

I shook my head to regain focus; Liam was speaking to me.

"Ever been inside before now?"

"No."

"And you thought it was beautiful?" He sauntered over.

"Well, from the outside."

He laughed and I rolled my eyes.

God, he loved to tease. He and Linea would get along well.

I paused. Why was I thinking that?

"Come on. I'll give you a tour."

"Oh, um, great."

I really should have been going home. I'd come here wanting to get to know Liam better. And I had, while having a nice, casual dinner with him.

I could make my assessment of his character later, when I was in the quiet of my own home. Where I should be headed right now.

Instead, my feet followed him. The need to be near him won out over anything else. Linea would groan in frustration if she saw me now.

Thank goodness I was here alone with Liam.

Liam led me down a short walkway, opening doors to different rooms. Everything was clean and in its proper place, but it was sterile, like the rooms were hardly used.

"You were an only child," I stated more than asked.

He paused on his way out of what used to be the drawing room. "Yes."

"How did you and your parents deal with so many empty rooms?"

His eyes took on a faraway look that indicated fond memories. "When I was younger, it was great for hide and seek. On weekends, my parents would host parties for friends. But as I grew older, I ended up spending most of my time at your dad's."

"That's lovely."

His eyes held mine and his mouth twitched. "Yes, it was."

When we finished looking at the rooms downstairs, we headed up to the second floor.

"There are five bedrooms with three baths."

"Wow." My eyes widened. "That's big."

"Didn't feel like such a big deal when it was built, I'm sure. Times are different now."

"I know," I murmured, thinking of my tiny apartment that I could walk through in two minutes.

On the contrary, I could get lost in this house.

Liam pointed to a door. "Bedroom one." He kept moving and pointing them out. "They're all the same thing. Four-poster beds, dressers, the works."

He pushed a door open for me to see. "My parents wanted to maintain the integrity of the old home."

"And you want that, too?"

"Yeah." He scrunched his face. "Kind of. I won't touch the inside, but I'm adding a deck in the back and there's the clinic, so..."

I smiled and pointed to a door. "What's that one?"

"That's my room."

It'd been great seeing the house so far, but this would be the icing on the cake. "Oh, Dr. Cooper, I'm curious to see where you sleep."

His chest rumbled with laughter. "It's very basic. You'll be disappointed." He pushed open the door and let me pass.

My brows lifted as I took in the space. Light curtains covered the windows and the floor had a soft rug. His bed was a king-sized four-poster and there was a nightstand with a reading lamp.

What struck me, though, was its similarity with the rest of the house. Everything was spick-and-span.

"Do you sleep here?" I spun to him.

He shrugged. "Yes, why?"

"Um, hello? It looks—" I made my way in, turning in a circle, looking for something out of place "—too clean."

"Is that bad?"

"No, I guess I'm just so used to seeing messy homes. It's almost like a no one lives here."

Liam prowled toward me, his gaze dark. "Do I look like no one?"

I couldn't tear my gaze away from his. "No, I just meant…" I licked my lips and his eyes followed the movement.

My blood turned to liquid heat in my veins. Probably the pregnancy hormones had me horny as hell.

Having sex with Liam wasn't why I came here.

I took in a shaky breath. "I should go."

Yet, my feet wouldn't budge.

Liam took a step closer and lined up his front with mine. His hand lifted and swept across my cheek tenderly.

My eyes fell shut, body trembling.

"You should stay," he rasped, "maybe get *dirty* with me in my room."

Then his mouth covered mine.

I wrapped my hands around his neck, winding my fingers in his hair and pulling him closer.

He groaned and wrapped firm hands around my hips, pulling me harder against him and grinding.

His length pressed against my stomach, but I wanted to taste him.

"Sit," I said, my voice shaky.

Just as he sat, I got on my knees.

No belt buckle got in my way today. It was sinful how this man made sweatpants look sexy. I pulled them down, my breath rushing out of me.

Liam's hard cock filled my hand and I stroked. His body tensed, a groan coming from his lips.

I hadn't even begun yet.

Keeping my eyes on his, I licked the underside of his cock. The crown beaded with precum and I rolled my tongue around it. The salty flavor burst on my tongue and I moaned.

"Fuck." Liam bucked, thrusting deeper into my mouth.

I shivered. Since the last time we were together, this was all I could think about. And now I was savoring it.

Going all in, I wrapped both hands around the base and took him deeper.

"Fuck, Ava." He swept my hair back, rutting deeper into my throat. "Feels so good. I don't want to hurt you. Can't help it. Feels—ahh, fuck."

My core clenched. Giving him pleasure gave me pleasure.

I felt powerful making him lose his composure.

As I stroked the base of his cock, I continued to lick and suck Liam into my mouth. I snaked one hand between my thighs and stroked my aching clit.

A moan escaped my throat, and he groaned at the sensation.

"I want to come inside you, Ava." Liam pulled me up. "Sit on my cock—ride daddy's cock."

A tingle danced down my spine, setting my core on fire. I quickly kicked off my sandals and slid my panties off.

I skipped taking off my dress; I didn't want to wait any longer.

Liam didn't mind. He collected me into his arms as I straddled him.

"That's a good girl," he murmured as his cock grazed my folds.

I moaned, burying my face in his neck. My hips circled his dick, searching for the tip, yearning to be filled. "I want you inside me, daddy."

"How could I say no to my baby girl?" he growled as he drove into me.

My cry echoed through the bedroom. Whimpers and moans followed as Liam thrust into me.

His hands on my hips kept me steady, the sound of our bodies slapping together filling the space.

A tingle started in my lower belly. "Daddy, I think I'm going to come."

"Fuck, so soon?" His movements turned shaky.

He moved one hand between us to stroke my clit. "That's it, Ava. Take daddy's cock."

His words drove me wild. Bracing my hands on his shoulders, I rolled my hips, chasing my orgasm.

"That's right. Come all over my cock," Liam cooed.

My body seized up, then I exploded. I couldn't stop the keening wail that escaped my lips.

Liam's shaft felt so full inside me as I pulsed around him.

"So good," I cried.

He kissed my lips hard as he filled me with his cum. Heat flooded my depths and I came again.

He murmured a curse but didn't let up. He cupped my face and his lips softened, kissing me tenderly.

When my limbs turned weak, I sagged against him.

He held me close and stroked my hair softly. "Should we—"

"Do it again?" I offered.

"I was going to say take off our clothes," he chuckled.

"We can do both."

Chapter 12

Liam

I stirred awake, my eyes opening slowly. The sheets were rumpled and one of the pillows was nowhere to be found. That never happened.

I usually slept peacefully and woke up to everything in its place.

But that wasn't the case last night. Last night was wild and messy. In a delicious way that left my muscles a tad sore but very much sated.

I blinked against the sunshine, searching for the woman who rode me like I was the last cowboy in the world.

Rolling over, I found her rising from the bed.

My cock twitched at the sight of her.

Every inch of her body was perfection. From her luscious ass to the swell of her breasts. Her back flexed as she stretched her arms above her head.

A smile curved my lips.

She turned slightly. The morning light from the

window poured over her face, tits, and the swell of her backside.

She reached up to shake out her mussed hair and I swallowed.

So beautiful.

The most beautiful thing I'd ever seen.

"You're beautiful," I whispered.

She turned with a bright smile, her face flushed. "You're awake."

"Mm-hmm." I nodded. "Were you trying to sneak out before I woke up?"

"I wasn't. I-I just…" Her eyes met mine and mischief danced in them. "Yeah, that's exactly what I was doing."

I let my gaze roam over her. "You weren't very successful, then."

"No, I guess I wasn't." She wrapped an arm around her breasts and covered her center with a hand.

"Don't bother trying to cover yourself. It's all imprinted here." I tapped the side of my head. "But just in case, why don't you come here and refresh my memory."

Her laughter tinkled across my senses. "Nice try. I'm not climbing back into bed."

She backed away, bending down, looking for something.

"Are you sure? I can make it worth your while."

Laughing, she gave up and knelt down, searching under the bed. "Where's my bra?"

I thought for a second. All that crossed my mind from last night was the feel of her skin on mine.

Neither of us had paid attention to where our clothes dropped, as long as they were off our bodies.

"Check at the foot of the bed," I offered.

She rounded to my side. "Found it."

Before she could leave, I palmed her ass. She yelped and skipped away, pulling a laugh from me.

Bra found, she laid the rest of her clothes on the bed and started to get dressed.

My lengthened cock and I mourned every inch of her skin hidden by her clothes.

"What time is it?"

I groped around the nightstand and found my phone. I blinked blearily at the screen before my eyes managed to focus. When I read out the hour, Ava jumped.

"Oh, God. I need to get going. I've got a house appointment in half an hour and if I don't get there on time, Linea will never let me hear the end of it."

"Sounds ominous."

"Oh, she can be." She tried to smile but her attention was on zipping up her dress.

"Can I help?"

Whatever she heard in my tone made her eye me. "You won't drag me back to bed, right?"

"Pinky promise."

Her brows furrowed as she sat on the bed beside me. "Seriously? Pinky promise?"

"It's a long story." I kissed her back before drawing up her zipper. "I'll tell you next time."

She was silent for so long before she asked, "Next time?"

I rose on an elbow, taking her face in. "Yes. When can I see you again?"

Ava stood at the foot of the bed, a smile playing across her lips. "When do you want to see me again?"

I thought for a second. "Tonight."

If possible, I wouldn't let her leave. We'd spend the whole of today together. But that wasn't possible since we both had to work.

The next best option was to see her this evening.

Her eyes widened, like she wasn't sure what to say.

"Come over." I sat up. The covers fell, exposing my upper body.

Her eyes ate me up, throat bobbing as she visibly swallowed. The way she sucked me into her mouth so eagerly last night came back and my cock thickened.

I wanted to return the favor.

"Let me take care of you after your long day of cleaning. What do you say?"

Her eyes brightened. "I think I like the sound of that."

My phone beeped and she resumed getting dressed. She sat and pulled on her sandals.

"So, I'll be here at seven. Is that okay?"

I nodded.

"Okay." Her eyes held mine for a second, smile bright.

She stood, straightening her dress. "It's my turn to prepare a dish for a family in need."

"Are they alright?" I frowned.

"Mostly. Just overwhelmed and stretched thin because they just had triplets." She squirmed. "Can you imagine that?"

I chuckled. "One child is a lot. But three? Wow."

She bit her lip. "Yeah, babies are a lot to handle."

Her sad look unfurled something inside me. I stood and rounded the bed to pull her into my arms. She melted against me, sighing.

"You're doing a great job, Ava. I'm sure everyone appreciates what you can offer."

"Thank you." Her voice came out muffled.

I let her go so I could cup her face. Warm eyes blinked up at me. I kissed her lips softly.

Her palms flattened on my chest as she kissed me back.

"You have to get to work, right?" I murmured.

"Shoot."

But she didn't pull away. If anything, she was clinging to me more.

"Shoot is right," I said in a teasing tone.

That snapped her out of it. She stepped back and eyed me but her lips twitched.

"I should go."

I'll miss you.

I swallowed those words and said instead, "I'd like to help with what you do."

Her eyes widened. "You want to cook or do grocery shopping for families in need?"

I nodded.

A big smile covered her face. "Oh, okay. I'll add you to the rotation." She looked around the room before facing me. "I have to go."

"Okay."

We shared one more kiss before I could let her out the door.

Then I dropped onto the bed and counted to one hundred so I wouldn't go downstairs and ask her to stay.

IT WAS a busy day at the clinic. Patients trickled in, one after the other. There wasn't a dull moment.

But despite all of this, my head found a way to make space for Ava. In between listening to complaints and prescribing medication, I pictured her smile, heard her laughter, and felt her touch.

A persisting thought that forced its way into that sweet fantasy was my friend's face.

What would he think about me and Ava together?

I could almost picture his face changing from his usual

quick smile to a hard frown. It reminded me of the Thomas I used to know.

"You okay, Doc?" Mr. Harold raised a brow.

He'd come for his checkup without his daughter —surprisingly.

"I'm great."

"You seem distracted. Your woman giving you trouble?"

I chuckled. "No, sir. I don't have a woman."

"Hard to believe."

I shook my head and read through his chart. "Everything looks good. The wound healed up nicely and I guess I won't be seeing you for a while."

"So, you looking for a wife?"

"No—"

"My daughter is a good woman. Has two sons and is married to a doofus of a man, but a divorce can be arranged."

I laughed. "No need, Mr. Harold."

"There's that laugh." He grinned. "Now you're more like yourself."

A shocked sound left me. Did he just try to get me to loosen up? The grumpy old man?

"I'll be taking my old bones away now, Doc." He eased off the exam table and adjusted his hat. "Keep that smile on, okay?"

I could do nothing but assent.

As I saw more patients, I stayed in the present, for their sake. Yet, Thomas's possible reaction to what I had with Ava bugged me to no end.

He'd be mad for sure, but what would he do about it?

The Thomas I knew threw punches first and asked questions later. At least, he was that way when we were kids. It was great when he was defending me, but now?

Would he see me as a threat to Ava? Throw punches to protect her?

I rubbed my jaw. I wasn't looking forward to any of that. He had a mean right hook.

And just because he owned a grocery store and wore cardigans didn't diminish that. He was the kid who fiercely protected those he loved.

It was in him.

And I was sure he wouldn't hesitate to unleash it on me.

"Dr. Cooper?" My nurse's voice pulled me out of my thoughts.

She frowned like she'd been there a while.

I grimaced. "Yes?"

"It's time for lunch. We're ordering Chinese. Want some?"

I smiled. "Yeah, sure."

She smiled back. "Okay."

Once I was alone again, I looked at my watch. In a few hours, I'd see Ava again.

A rush went through me. It was unusual for me to feel this way about a woman. I looked forward to nothing more than holding her in my arms and talking.

She was becoming very special to me. I didn't want to keep us a secret. I wanted to be able to tell Mr. Harold that I had a special woman in my life.

Maybe I'd broach the subject with her tonight. We'd go public. Let her dad know before he found out on his own.

The chicken chow mein tasted as good as last night's, but it wasn't the same without Ava.

I resumed work but couldn't keep my eyes off the clock. In my old life, that meant I was exhausted and just needed to sleep.

But my body thrummed today. I wanted the pleasure

of being with Ava, having her next to me. 7 p.m. couldn't come quick enough.

Yet, thoughts of Thomas doused my excitement to see her. He wouldn't like me being with his daughter.

The decision to tell him, and put it out in the open didn't seem so alluring now. But it was the right thing to do.

But what if we did keep it to ourselves? What he didn't know wouldn't hurt him. He'd be blissfully unaware and Ava and I could explore this thing between us.

My stomach coiled. What was I thinking?

Could I justify prioritizing my desire for Ava over doing the right thing by Thomas?

I still didn't have the answer by quitting time. But at least I could look forward to seeing Ava tonight.

Chapter 13

Ava

It was almost 7 p.m. when I stopped outside Liam's house.

Leaving this morning was hard and I'd looked forward to coming back all day. Linea teased me mercilessly until I told her the truth.

Great sex wasn't what had me excited to see him again, though. It was more than just sex now. I enjoyed his company. It was about *him*.

I took a deep breath and wiped my forehead. I'd rushed through preparing a meal for the couple with triplets and had made myself a bit winded.

Even through their front door, I could hear three high-pitched cries. The mom's baggy eyes and tired smile greeted me as she collected the meal. As the new dad appeared next to her, I saw his eyes were lined with dark circles, too.

"Are you guys okay?" I asked. Damn, they looked so...exhausted.

"We'll survive," the mom said.

"Thank you, Ava." The dad nodded his head slightly before pulling his wife back inside.

I stood and stared at their front door, listening to the babies' cries.

Is this what my life would become?

Now in the car outside Liam's, I covered my stomach with a hand. "Don't be a fussy baby, please."

Or fussy *babies*?

No way. I was only having one child.

One child is a lot.

Liam's voice echoed in my head. I sighed heavily.

I needed to tell the man at some point. Let him know that our child—please, let it only be one—would be born soon.

Not too soon. It was likely at least eight months away.

I looked at my dashboard. Two minutes to seven.

Why was I out here stalling? I'd looked forward to seeing Liam all day. Now, a shaky feeling pooled in my belly.

Like a teenage girl having her first crush.

My face flushed and I pushed myself out of the car, shut the door, and locked it.

I wasn't crushing on Liam. I was getting to know him for the sake of our child.

Refusing to think more about that, I climbed up the steps and knocked. A few seconds passed before the door opened.

I gulped back the sigh that rose in my chest. Liam was dressed in a blue button-down shirt that molded to his frame. It flowed into dark blue dress pants and black dress shoes.

My eyes flicked back to his face, making a quick note of the buttons opened at his throat.

That shaky feeling turned into full-on butterflies.

I said the first thing that came to mind. "Are we going out?"

Please don't say yes.

Compared to his business apparel, I'd thrown on a pair of jeans and a casual top, along with boots.

"No, we're staying in." His lip quirked up. "Please, come in."

I couldn't help my smile. I walked past him into his beautiful home and waited as he shut the door.

His hand rested on the small of my back, steering me. "How was your day?"

Shivers edged down my spine. A voice as silky and deep as his should be criminal.

I blinked a few times to clear my head. He'd asked me a question.

"Um, it was great. Linea and I cleaned three houses. They were all polished and tidy when we were done."

"That's lovely."

I looked up and our eyes met. His carried an intensity that told me he meant every word spoken.

I swallowed. So what if my job wasn't glamorous? We didn't save lives, but what we did made a difference.

But I wasn't about to bring all that up.

"How was yours?"

"I saw quite a few patients. Some grumpy, some excitable. It was all good."

I wanted to say more, but we had made it to the dining room and I lost my voice.

The heavy curtains on the north wall were pushed aside and revealed floor to ceiling windows.

The evening sky was stark and beautiful. I felt like I was under the stars right now.

"I noticed you liked sitting outside last night." Liam's

voice was tight. "This is the closest we can have without the chill."

My heart squeezed. I turned to him and an unsure look crossed his eyes. Was he worried that I didn't like it?

I smiled. "It's lovely."

Leaving his side, I crossed the room, closer to the window, and soaked it in. "Beautiful."

After a few moments, I turned.

For the first time, my eyes took in the room.

The dining table was covered in silver-plated dishes. Candles burned on different surfaces in the room, lending the space a warm feel.

"Liam, this is…" My eyes met his. "Wow."

"It's just dinner." He waved me over. "Come on."

I rounded the table big enough to seat six people comfortably to the spot where he stood. He pulled out the chair so I could sit.

Then he took the one opposite me.

My eyes ran over the dishes. "Did you make all of these?"

He nodded.

My face heated. *Okay.*

Suddenly shy, I turned away, pushing my hair behind my ear. He'd done all this for me?

I wasn't used to men going to so much trouble for me. Certainly not the guys I'd dated in the past.

Liam may be older than me, but he had…everything going for him. He was an amazing lover, cleaned, cooked, and set a table like a five-star restaurant!

"This is for you."

I turned and smiled, collecting the single red rose. Its smell tickled my nose. "Thank you."

He smiled back. "Shall we eat?"

It took a few minutes to decide what I wanted to try

first. But once I tasted the beef stew, I wanted a bite of everything he'd cooked.

"How did you learn to cook so well if you never had much time?"

"It was one thing I did with my parents. Making dinner. It was a whole affair."

I bit my lip. What if Liam and I could have that with our child? Little moments to bond as a family.

"Wine?" He lifted a bottle over the glass next to my plate.

"Sure." The word came out before I considered it.

I couldn't have wine. It was alcohol and that was bad for the baby.

Dr. Morris said I could have a drink here and there, but how much was that? I didn't want to take a chance with my baby's health.

But my glass was already filled with red wine.

I just wouldn't drink it.

Liam picked up his glass by the stem. "To a lovely dinner with a beautiful woman."

My heart melted.

"Let's have a toast, Ava."

Oh, yeah.

I grabbed my wine and raised the glass. "To a lovely dinner with a beautiful man."

"How did I know you'd say that?" His eyes crinkled with laughter.

We clinked glasses and I placed the cool rim on my lips. He was looking at me, so I tipped it.

I tried not to cringe and placed the glass on the table. That was a tiny sip. No more now.

Liam's gray eyes followed every single thing I did, including my wine aversion. "You don't like it?"

He'd almost finished his first glass, and I'd barely drunk from mine.

"No, it's great. I'm just not much of a wine drinker."

"Oh." Liam's brows lifted.

I inwardly winced. I loved wine, just not right now. "Yeah."

"But you like beer, right? I'll get you a beer."

"No!" I protested a little too loud.

I held onto his arm to keep him from standing.

"No?"

"No. I don't want you to leave." True enough.

His eyes looked doubtful.

Think, Ava.

"I want to hear the pinky promise story."

The wary look in his eyes turned to a smile and his body relaxed. Only then did I pull my hand back.

"My first patient after I finished medical school was a little girl. She had a broken pinky finger. It got smashed in a window."

"Sounds horrible."

"It was." His brows knotted, like he could still picture it. "She kept saying she won't be able to make promises and keep them anymore since she couldn't use her pinky."

"Aww…" A sad laugh left my lips. "What about her other pinky?"

"It had to be the right one."

"Well, did it ever get better?"

He nodded. "In a few weeks she was alright. Since then —" his eyes met mine "—my pinky promises are my most serious promises."

"That's sweet."

He smiled ruefully.

We returned to the meal, and I prayed he'd forgotten about the beer.

When our plates were clear of dessert, I hopped to my feet, relieved. "I'll help you clean this up."

We stocked the fridge with the leftovers. Liam insisted on washing the dishes himself.

When he was done, he took my hand. My eyes narrowed, but I followed his lead.

He took us upstairs, past all the empty rooms, to his bedroom. Seeing the space where we'd made love last night had my body on fire.

But Liam didn't stop by the bed. He walked straight through to the bathroom. It was pristine, unsurprisingly, and had a giant tub.

"You must be tired." He stopped by the door, taking in my face.

His hands didn't caress my skin, but I felt him everywhere.

"I'll run us a bath. You must be sore after the long day you've had. Take off your clothes."

My breath caught in my throat. I moved into the bedroom to do as he asked.

My hands shook with every button I unfastened.

The light from the bathroom spilled out, and I looked up. Liam was undoing his cuffs and buttons, but his eyes were on me.

We watched each other get undressed. And with every inch of his skin that was revealed, my center grew a little wetter.

I was ready to put a fingertip there to ease the ache, but he reached for my hand.

In the steaming bathroom, he helped me into the tub, and a gasp left me. It was hot; almost too hot.

I leaned against the side, my muscles relaxing in the heated bath. It felt so good.

Liam got in the other end, and I glimpsed his hard

length before he sank under the water. His arms rested on both sides of the tub, his chest wide and strong.

My pulse quaked. In my neck, my tummy, my center.

The water felt good, maybe a little too hot due to my pregnancy hormones. What I really wanted, though, was to be in Liam's arms.

He leaned his head back and closed his eyes, exposing his glorious muscles. His Adam's apple bobbed, and the sudden need to lick his neck clutched my insides.

Before I could talk myself out of it, I moved toward him.

My thighs brushed his, and his eyes opened, head tilting up to look at me. Biting my lip, I crawled onto his lap.

A moan fell from my lips as my center grazed his shaft. I bobbed in the water, rubbing my folds against the underside.

Liam groaned and wrapped his arms around me, flattening my body against his chest. I licked his throat, tasting a hint of floral bath wash and a unique taste that was all his.

I kissed his smooth jawline all the way to his ear. His mouth claimed mine then, a sharp exhale leaving him.

Firm hands wrapped up in my damp hair, his tongue finding mine. I held onto his shoulders, giving myself over to his kisses, his touch, his everything.

Nothing had ever felt this good.

His hands moved down to my hips, helping me to rub against him better.

A whimper left my throat. I was so close. I moved faster, reaching for that elusive high.

Water sloshed over the tub's edges, and our quick pants filled the space.

"Liam," I whispered into his mouth.

He kissed me fervently, rubbing the head of his cock through my folds. "What do you need, Ava?"

"I want—" *gasp* "—more."

He squeezed my ass, teasing me one last time before withdrawing.

"Why did you stop?" I complained.

"Hey, hey," Liam brushed my hair away and cupped my face, then kissed my lips. "Let's go to bed, okay?"

A thrill ran through me. "Okay."

Chapter 14

Liam

Water dripped from Ava's sleek form onto the bathroom floor. I got out after her and grabbed two towels, wrapping her up in one. She draped it over her shoulders, then moved toward the bedroom.

"Are you coming?"

Bewitched by her voice and the sexy glint in her eyes, I nodded. "Go wait for me."

Ava's naked body flashed me as she handed the towel over and went to the bedroom.

My cock expanded, and precum dripped from the tip, wanting to sink into her right this minute.

But we had all night. There was no rush.

I toweled off and headed in to join her. The sight that hit my eyes turned my breath hot.

Ava lay in the middle of the bed with her knees drawn up. Her hands were on her breasts, fingers playing with her nipples.

One moment I was by the door, and the next, I found myself kneeling between her legs.

"You drive me crazy, Ava," I groaned. My throat was so tight.

"You drive me crazy, too." And as if wanting to show me how much, she squeezed her nipples and moaned. Her back arched off the bed, her pelvis lifting so she brushed against my cock.

A growl ripped from my chest. I fell onto one arm, staring between us as she started to grind her slit on my length.

"Liam, I can't help it. I need you."

Fuck, that always got me.

"Okay, Ava. Lie back; let me pleasure you."

She sighed, closing her eyes and sinking back against the sheets, keeping her legs open wide for me.

I ran my fingers up and down her outer thighs, feeling the warmth of her skin on my palms.

Her soft moan carried through the room.

I wanted more of that sound.

Leaning forward, I kissed her lips.

She didn't expect that. Her eyes cracked open and held mine. It took a second, but she responded with a deep kiss.

I tasted dinner and lust and *her*, all tangled together in a heady mix. My blood pumped with need.

I cupped her face and kissed her deeper until she clawed my back in a plea for more. I broke away, looking down at her. Ava's hands snatched me back.

Groaning, I dropped down and lined my cock along her damp folds. I thrust once, and she cried against my mouth. Her hips tilted, attempting to pull me inside.

"Liam…"

It would be so easy to take her now. She was panting and needy. But I wanted to give her everything.

Even if it meant denying my own need.

I drew back, and her hips speared off the bed, following me.

"Ava," I grabbed her waist, steadying her. "Be patient."

"No," she whined. "I want you now."

"You'll have me. Just be patient, okay, princess?"

She nodded reluctantly, tossing her head to the side, eyes fluttering closed. Her hips settled back on the bed, but the slight tremors in her limbs made it clear her pause was only temporary.

I kissed her neck, and she sighed, exposing more of herself for me. Her soft skin tasted sweet as I licked and sucked.

Decadent.

I licked a path down to her breasts, then cupped one, pinching and pulling gently on her nipple while I lapped at the other. Her pink nipples hardened with my attention.

Every tug had her mewling, her lithe body dancing off the bed.

"Oh, God, Liam," she cried. "Please."

I moved lower to her belly button. Her stomach quivered, and I gave it a little kiss, moving lower to her soaking wet pussy. She was primed and ready for me.

She thrust her hips in small pumps that made my cock jerk, hungry to sink in.

I clenched my jaw, ignoring the heavy pulse in my cock. Not yet.

I traced my tongue down to the little bud at the top of her folds. Ava gasped, her hands fisting in my hair, holding on tight.

Closing my eyes, I settled my hands underneath her ass cheeks and tilted her up slightly. I wanted to taste everything.

She tasted so fucking good, and my cock grew impatient, thrusting against the sheets as my upper lip and chin became wet from licking her.

Ava's cries turned into a steady whine. Her body shook under me, and her hands yanked at my hair. But I felt nothing but pleasure.

Every movement, every sound, caused need to swell inside me. My breath rasped out, my voice cutting the air in a low growl.

"Open up for me, Ava."

She whimpered, trying to keep her thighs apart. "It's too much. I-I want to come."

I returned my attention to her sweet pussy. With my tongue on her clit, I worked one finger between her folds, caressing and teasing.

"Liam!" she cried, hips rising.

I brought my left hand up and placed it on her stomach, keeping her steady. She trembled under my touch, fingers digging into my scalp.

Her neediness spurred me on.

Stroking my index and middle finger through her wet heat, I drew her clit between my lips, then sank my fingers into her clenching core.

"Oh, fuck. Oh, Liam!"

"Steady," I groaned against her clit, and kept lapping up her cream. "You wanna come?"

"So bad." She punctuated the words with two firm pelvic thrusts against my fingers.

"Alright. In a minute, my sweet girl."

I knew Ava's body, what she needed. Pushing my head in closer, I returned to her clit and bit gently. Her shuddering cry was response enough.

I zeroed in on that spot while gently fucking my fingers in and out of her. Her clench grew firmer, and her body stilled its motions.

"Right there, right there," she cried.

"Here?" I curved my fingers and stroked her deep.

Her body surged up, shaking. "Liam, oh, fuck!"

I kept up my motions even as tremors passed through her body and she bucked into my face. She came for a long moment, until boneless, she dropped onto the bed.

Only then did I work my fingers out and lift my head.

Ava watched me with brown eyes, still dark with lust. "You…" she gasped as another shockwave passed through her.

I smirked and dipped her fingers into my mouth, licking them clean.

Ava's tongue darted out to lick her lower lip.

"Want to taste yourself, Ava?" Her hungry eyes ate me up. "Come get it."

She was already on her knees, reaching for my neck. Her soft body melted against mine as she kissed me. A soft moan left her lips, vibrating through me.

"How do you taste? Tell me." My voice came out hoarse.

"Like I'm ready to be fucked."

My cock surged, pressing into her stomach.

She paused, eyes meeting mine before her hand went between us.

I groaned as fingers wrapped around me, stroking slowly.

"You're hard as steel, daddy."

My hips jerked, driving my cock into her touch. "Fuck, Ava."

"Want me to fix that?"

I took in her wide eyes, her mussed hair, and her swollen red lips. I nodded, not trusting myself to speak.

She smiled before tonguing down my body just like I'd

done to hers. Her lips grazed my flat nipples, and strange pleasure slid down my spine.

"Ava."

"Hmm?" she answered lightly before continuing.

Her kiss went to the muscles of my abs.

My eyes fell shut, my limbs tightening. I couldn't breathe until her mouth was on me.

She took her sweet time, licking the V-line of my abdomen, the tops of my thighs, and everything but my cock itself.

"Damn it, Ava," I growled. "Get your mouth on me."

"Maybe you should feed it to me."

My eyes flickered open, looking down. She'd let go of my cock and was bent at the waist. Her sweet ass was sticking up in the air, but it was her slightly open mouth just at my cock's head that had my breath coming faster.

"What are you waiting for, daddy? I'm thirsty and I want to drink your cum."

I fisted my cock, stroking roughly before guiding it between her sweet, soft lips.

"Fucking hell," I groaned.

Her sucking mouth took over, pulling me deeper until her lips closed around the base.

Heat threaded through my body. "You look so beautiful taking my cock so deep."

A smile lit her eyes, and she began to move.

My lower back tightened, breath punching out of me. I fisted a hand in her hair and fought the need to thrust away.

She looked happy taking me slow and steady. I wasn't about to be a greedy bastard and push her more than she could handle.

So instead of putting my hand on her head and

pressing deeper, I ran my hand through her hair, massaging.

"You're doing a good job, baby. Keep making daddy proud."

Those words pleased her. She moaned around my dick, sucking deeper.

I didn't miss the hand she sent between her thighs to stroke herself. Or how her movements turned faster, more urgent.

Hell, I wanted this to go on forever, but I needed to be inside her, too.

"Get on your back for me, Ava."

Her mouth popped off my cock, and she drew a ragged breath, lying on her back.

I knelt between her thighs and, without a moment's pause, pressed my cock into her sweet, wet pussy.

My eyes begged to close in pleasure as I sank the first inch in. But Ava's eyes were wide open, holding mine.

Her lips were wet and swollen from sucking my cock. Her hair fanned out around her face.

She was the sexiest sight I'd ever beheld, and I kept my gaze on her as I stroked into her slowly, inch by inch.

Her chest rose and fell faster, her eyes growing heavier.

"Liam," she gasped as I bottomed out.

My breath scraped out. "Oh, Ava."

I fell on my elbows so I could kiss her lips. Her hands flattened on my shoulders, and her legs wrapped around my lower back, her heels digging into my backside.

Impossibly, she took me deeper. "Liam, you make me feel so good."

Her voice lost its edge, turning smoky with need.

"Me too," I whispered right before we kissed.

I moved inside her, awed by it all. We were joined at the hips, at our lips. But something tugged deeper in my chest, something that was always there, but was growing stronger.

It made me want to hold her close. Always have her here with me. In my bed, every night.

Maybe not even fucking, as I did now, taking her with rough thrusts. I'd be happy just holding her, making her feel safe and cared for.

And really feel me.

The way I felt her.

"Ava," I murmured.

Her eyes opened and caught mine. Whatever she saw in them made her gaze turn soft, and she kissed me, running her hands through my hair.

I kissed her back, tangling our tongues.

It didn't take long for her hips to start meeting mine, her breath turning ragged.

"Liam, I think I'm—"

"I know, baby."

A shudder rocked her body. "Please, make me come, daddy."

I kissed her neck and angled my thrusts to hit her sweet spot just right. That seemed to chase away any last restraint she had.

Her cries filled the room, rivaled only by the slap of our bodies coming together.

"Liam, I'm coming. You're making me—"

Her pussy fisted mine tightly as her pleasured cry rang out. I tried to keep going, prolong her pleasure, but it was too good.

Two hard pumps and I spilled into her, groaning into her neck. "Fuck, you take me so well, Ava. What a good girl."

She moaned, still squirming under me. I held steady, emptying my balls until the tremors eased.

Strength left me. I fell to my side and drew her against my chest, wrapping her up in a hug. She felt so right there.

Maybe it was the shared pleasure. But the feeling didn't ebb as her breathing turned heavy, and my eyelids drooped.

No, it was more than the sex. I wanted her here.

I had to tell Thomas, and soon. Not that I fucked his daughter. But that I wanted her in my life.

I looked down at her lovely face, and my heart squeezed. Yes, I wanted her by my side.

My friend would be mad, and those famed punches would likely come, but for Ava, it would be worth it.

Chapter 15

Ava

Dad was in the kitchen putting the final touches on his new recipe. It amused me how each recipe that involved rice and chicken could be considered new. But I was hungry and obviously not going to complain.

I'd been hungry a lot lately. I smiled down at my body but reminded myself not to touch my stomach while around Dad. He was too observant and I didn't want to raise his suspicion.

I resumed setting the table, and my eyes went to the space Liam had occupied the one time he'd joined us. A smile framed my lips, and I ran my fingers over the back of the chair.

Maybe Dad could invite him again. We'd be able to hide our connection.

I snorted. Who was I kidding?

In the last few days, Liam and I had grown closer. I always found my way to his home after work. One look at my tired face and he'd run a bath or mineral soak for us.

Then he'd prepare the most delicious dinners. After we ate, we'd call it a night and turn in.

If it were only sex, it'd be easy to pinpoint why he wanted me around.

But sometimes, he'd turn me down with, "You need to rest."

True, but I wanted him more than anything, even necessary bodily functions, like sleep.

No relationship, or whatever it was we had, had ever made me feel this much. No one had ever shown me such care, such tenderness.

At first, it confused me, maybe even scared me. I was worried about getting carried away. But as the days passed, he was steady as a rock.

Or was even more attentive.

I took my phone out and read the last text he sent. Just a simple checking-in message, but it warmed me inside.

He was present. So considerate. And we didn't even have a label yet.

I imagined how he'd be with his child. I couldn't resist rubbing my belly. He'd make a great dad.

"It's all done."

I whisked my hand away and turned to my dad. "Your rice and chicken."

Dad grinned, placing the platter on the table. "I know you're skeptical. But trust that aroma."

I sniffed the air, and hunger clawed at my stomach. "Okay, you win. It smells delicious."

Dad retrieved a jug of fresh juice from the fridge. Thank heavens, I wouldn't have to make up excuses why I didn't want wine. I could just relax and eat.

He settled in, and we dished out the food.

The first spoonful had my eyes shutting in appreciation.

"Good?"

"The best," I gushed. "Why didn't you tell me it was so tasty?"

"I did. You didn't trust me."

"I'll never doubt you, ever again," I added more food to my plate and dug in.

We were halfway through when I looked up at Dad. He'd been just dad my whole life, with his knit sweaters and big square glasses. Liam's story about his early dreams came into my memory, and my curiosity grew.

"What was becoming a father like for you?"

His eyes shot to mine. "Oh, uh, it was good."

"Come on, Dad." I put my fork down and moved my plate away. "Tell me all about it."

"Really?" He raised an eyebrow.

I nodded.

Heaving a sigh, he dropped his fork and settled against his chair. His gaze turned up to the ceiling like the answers were hidden there.

Then he spoke. "I was confused at first. I didn't know what I was supposed to do. But I guess I grew into it."

"How did you feel when you found out Mom was pregnant?"

I'd always known I was a surprise baby. They didn't plan it, but Dad hardly ever spoke about it. Not at all like something he regretted.

"I was scared." His eyes grew distant, and he laughed. "Terrified. I was so young. Didn't know the first thing about kids or pregnancies."

His smile disappeared, eyes growing serious. "I worried I wouldn't be able to be there like I should for your mom."

"But you stayed."

"Yes." He shook his head, still lost in his thoughts. "There was no other choice. After the initial terror passed, it was your mom and me and the life we were bringing into this world. It was all I cared about."

Liam had said they were going to leave their hometown, but I came along, and my dad had to stay back. There was no way I could admit what I knew without tracing it back to Liam.

So I reframed the next question in my head. "What was the biggest adjustment you had to make?"

"Biggest?" A line appeared between his brows. "Learning how to function with little sleep after you were born."

"I think I was a good baby."

"A little terror, that's what you were."

I laughed. "What else?"

"A little firecracker. Hell, you could yell all night just for the sake of it."

"Dad, I meant what else did you have to adjust in your life."

"Oh." He grinned, then shrugged. "Just knowing my life was no longer all mine. You and your mom came first."

My heart clenched, and my hand shook with the need to touch my stomach. My baby came first, too, but I was afraid.

"Do you feel like you missed out on certain things?" I leaned forward.

His eyes bounced off me, turning upward. "Do I? Some things, yes. Like partying with the boys, going off to college, all of that."

"Oh."

"But do I regret not having those things? No." He looked at me, eyes soft. "Having you gave me direction and showed me what truly mattered. I could have whiled away time being stupid. But you taught me to grow up."

My eyes misted. "Dad…"

"It's true." He breathed out. "Heck, I don't know where I'd be now if not for your mom and you. But here is the place I want to be the most."

I smiled. "But Dad, did you ever wish things had happened differently?"

He scoffed a laugh. "No, Peanut. Life is just the way it should be. The only thing I wish for is that your mom was still here."

I dabbed at my eyes. He'd loved her, and even though I didn't know her, his stories let me love her, too.

"Me too, Dad."

His eyes crinkled with his smile. "So, are you done messing with my emotions?"

I thought for a second. "Yeah, pretty much."

Dad chuckled and resumed eating.

I returned to my plate, but I'd lost my appetite. One day, it'd be my child and me. And maybe Liam, too?

"So, why all these questions? Where are they coming from?"

I lifted my eyes to meet Dad's. Trying for nonchalance, I shrugged. "It's nothing. I'm just thinking about the future."

Dad didn't seem satisfied, so I went on.

"I've never thought I wanted kids so much, but now, that opinion is changing."

His face broke into a huge smile. "Really?"

"Um, I was only thinking about—"

"That would be the best thing ever." He cast his gaze about. "I can almost picture a little one running around on Sunday nights."

I tilted my head.

"I'll babyproof, I assure you. I think I still have tools somewhere in the attic." He moved to stand.

"Dad, are you going right now?"

His eyes lit up. "Oh, well. I just thought I might as well get started." He dropped back into his chair, a huge grin on his face.

Disbelief mingled with joy in my chest, and I found myself smiling back.

Dad's focus went back to his meal. "You know, Christmases will be magical again with a child around. They'll get all excited about Santa, and we could put up decorations. And Halloween, too. We'll get costumes…"

He went on, and I bit my lip, trying to contain my glee. If he was this excited over the prospect of a child, he might be more open to me being pregnant than I thought.

"But hold on a minute." He pinned me with a serious look. "Is there something you're not telling me?"

My stomach clenched, and my heart drummed against my ribs. "W-what would I be keeping from you?"

"Are you seeing someone? Is that why you're thinking of starting a family?"

I nearly exhaled my relief, but his suspicions were still very apparent. I wanted to wiggle my way out of this.

But I pushed away that thought. It'd be best if I started laying the foundation for the truth. One of these days, he was going to find out.

The more prepared he was, the better.

"I am…seeing someone."

His eyes brightened. "Why haven't I heard about this before now?"

I tried to smile. "It's new."

He exhaled. "My baby's growing up. Is it serious?"

I thought for a second.

"Can I meet him?"

You already know him.

"Dad," I said in a rush. "It's still new, and that'd be taking things too fast."

"Well." Dad's face fell. "Tell me about him. What does he do?"

"I will." I smiled. "When the time is right. Just not right now."

He rumbled a disagreeing sound but nodded. "I understand. Take your time."

One thing I didn't have. But I was grateful he stopped pushing it.

Done with the meal, Dad started gathering the dishes. I stood to help, but just as I did, I got lightheaded.

A cry left me, and I tipped backward.

Dad caught me just before I hit the floor. "Ava." His voice was tense. "Are you okay?"

I pressed a shaky hand to my forehead, closing my eyes, trying to steady myself. "I am. I just—"

Dad helped me to stand upright, and another wave of dizziness hit me. My knees buckled.

"Shit," Dad swore, dropping me into the chair.

"I'm okay," I whispered, my chest rising and falling.

Why is this happening?

I massaged my forehead and blinked against the blur before my eyes. Nothing helped.

"Come on. We're going to see a doctor."

My heart lurched. If we saw a doctor, he'd find out about my baby. "No, Dad, I'm fine."

I tried to stand again, but his hands caught me before I fell on my face.

"You're not." His voice was curt and strained. "Come on, Peanut."

My eyes were closed as I leaned heavily against him. But I knew we walked in the direction of the front door.

"Watch your step."

I held onto his arm with a shaky hand, peeled my eyes open, and descended the porch steps.

When we hit the flat driveway, Dad hurried us once more. We got in his car, and he pulled onto the street.

Weak to my bones, I leaned back against the headrest, eyes closed. I just needed my head to clear, then I'd be fine.

"Talk to me, Peanut. How are you feeling?"

I couldn't pretend anymore. "Not very good."

"I'm sorry," he muttered. "We'll soon be at the doctor's."

I wanted to say I'd be alright, but my mouth wouldn't form the words. All my attention turned to the life growing inside me.

Was something happening to my baby? Tears sprang to my eyes. Nothing could happen to my child.

Without caring, I ran a hand over my stomach. Dad must have been too carried away to notice.

Please be okay, baby.

"We're here," he announced.

I opened my eyes, and a gasp left me. I sat up as strength rushed into my body. Liam was the last doctor I wanted to see.

Dad was already out of the driver's side and opening my door. "Okay, Peanut. Just get out slowly."

"Dad, I'm fine." My voice came out shaky. "No need for a doctor."

He ignored my plea and took my hand. "Come on. Let's get you fixed up."

Dad pulled me out of the car and the door shut behind me. All my protests fell on empty ears as he led me, determination and worry etched in his features.

Fear crowded out the sick feeling roiling through me.

I was going to see Liam, and he'd likely find out the truth.

Chapter 16

Liam

I prodded the logs in the fireplace. They hissed and popped, their orange flames burning brighter. I added two more logs and they turned fiery red.

Satisfied, I made my way to the kitchen and grabbed a corkscrew and a bottle of wine. I popped the cork and filled a glass with the dark liquid.

Back in the living room, I opened a book and settled before the fire. It crackled, sending warmth and light across the area.

Perfect.

Except for the empty spot next to me. We'd only been together for a few days, but I wanted to share every moment with Ava.

She was at her dad's tonight and that was one engagement I wouldn't want her leaving for me. He was special to her. Each time he came up in conversation, her eyes glowed with adoration.

I smiled and grabbed my phone. It was a few minutes

before nine o'clock. I calculated when she would be back home so I could call and hear her voice. That was all I'd be getting tonight.

I scoffed at myself. I never cared for anything much outside of work, but now? Ava filled my every waking thought.

If wanting her so much was wrong, then I'd deal with the punishment. I could do nothing else.

With a sigh, I relaxed on the couch and raised the book. Getting lost in the latest murder mystery should afford me some distraction until I spoke with her again.

I picked up from where I'd left off the last time, bringing my glass to my lips.

A knock rattled the front door.

I shot off the sofa, my eyes going to the front of the house. I felt something wet on my feet.

I'd spilled my drink.

Thankfully, it didn't get on the book.

The knock sounded again. This time it was longer, more insistent.

I set both book and glass aside and hurried to the door. Whoever it was on the other side better need something important.

Before the next round of banging could come, I opened the door.

My eyes fell on Ava first, then on my friend. I blinked rapidly. Weren't they at his house, having dinner? What was going on?

"Thomas, Ava, what's going on?"

My racing heart calmed. And my eyes focused long enough to catch the sweat shining on Ava's forehead. She leaned heavily against Thomas, who had an arm snaked around her waist.

His worried eyes met mine. "Liam."

His tone was impatient.

Did he know something? Had she told him what was going on between us?

My heart started beating into my throat. I raised both hands. By the look on his face, I wasn't getting out of this unscathed.

"Thomas, I can explain."

He tore past me. "What? Ava's ill. You have to help her."

"I'm fine," Ava croaked in response.

The tone of her voice startled me. And her breath was labored and short.

I shut the door, forgetting everything I assumed. Their visit clearly had nothing to do with me.

"You're not fine." Thomas gritted out. "She's not." He faced me with Ava still hanging on. "Can you help her?"

The look in his eyes made sense now. He was troubled.

I drew closer to them and took in Ava's pale features. "What happened?"

"We were just having dinner. Things were going great, until we finished, and Ava stood up. She nearly fainted."

"I must have slipped."

"You didn't." His eyes met mine again. "She almost collapsed."

"Dad, I'm okay now. If you just——"

"Don't listen to her. She can't even stand on her own."

"I can." Ava pried herself away from her dad. "See?"

It lasted two seconds before she dropped onto the sofa cushion.

Thomas cursed and my chest tightened.

"You see?" Thomas pressed. "Take a look at her, please?"

I pushed around Thomas to where Ava sat, kneeling before her. "Ava?"

She peeled her hands from her face and looked at me with wide brown eyes. Her usual spark had dulled and she blinked slowly.

Fuck.

My training and years of working under stress taught me not to panic. No matter how close she was to my heart, I needed to maintain my composure and a clear head.

"Keep your eyes open for a moment."

She tried but they fell shut again.

"What do you think is wrong?" Thomas hovered over us. "Is she okay?"

His tense energy was rubbing off on me.

"I can't tell here. It'd be best to take her to an exam room and do a thorough checkup."

"Okay, anything you need." He backed away, watching as I helped Ava up.

If he wasn't present, I'd have swung her into my arms and cradled her against my chest. But wrapping my arm around her waist would have to do.

I led her on gently, allowing her to take small steps so I didn't rattle her and make it worse.

"You're doing great, Ava. Just a few steps and we'll be at the clinic, okay?"

I didn't miss how her body leaned against mine and her breathing became steady and calm.

"I'll wait here," Thomas called, reminding me of his presence.

"This shouldn't take long," I threw over my shoulder.

The hallway connecting the house to the clinic was mercifully short. Each slow step Ava managed shone the light on her weakened state, and worry crowded in my stomach.

I wanted to fix what was wrong so she returned to her usual cheery self. It gutted me to see her suffering.

It was dark in the clinic, so I flicked on the lights as we headed to the exam room. We saw only outpatients, and we were closed on Sundays.

But I didn't mind opening for Ava. I was glad Thomas had brought her to me. I would help her in any way I could.

I assisted her onto the exam table. Her hands hit the surface, straining as she settled onto it.

"Can you sit up?"

She nodded, then stopped, pressing a hand to her forehead.

"Headache?" It was hard to pry my hands away from her.

"Feeling dizzy," she murmured, then her eyes cracked open. "Wait, no, I'm fine. It's nothing."

"Ava, it's not nothing." I frowned, stepping away.

Why was she so against getting help? Was she worried about Thomas finding out about us?

"Your dad's not here. We can talk freely."

Her eyes went to the door. "Yeah, um, I guess."

"We'll check your blood pressure first, okay?" I grabbed the equipment and brought it to her side.

She sat still as I wrapped her arm up, then pumped the device. It took a minute, then the numbers were displayed on the small screen.

My stomach turned liquid. What the fuck?

"What? What is it?" Ava leaned in, looking from me to the monitor.

"Your blood pressure is low." *Too low*. But I wasn't about to frighten her.

I pulled the monitor away and set it aside. "Ava, is this the first time you've experienced dizziness?"

She hugged her arms around herself. "Um, yes."

Her eyes wouldn't meet mine.

I swallowed a breath, trying to calm myself. It wasn't unusual for patients to keep certain facts hidden. It was my job to piece together the clues and make a diagnosis.

But this wasn't just any patient. It was Ava. She had no reason to keep anything hidden from me.

Our biggest secret was right here—the two of us, together. And the person we should be careful around was out there, not in here with us.

"You need to be open with me, princess."

Her eyes met mine, softening.

"Just tell me the truth, okay?"

"Okay," she managed.

"So when did you last experience the dizziness?"

"A few weeks ago."

I frowned. "Anything else unusual going on with you?"

Her fingers trailed up her thigh and formed a fist close to her hip. "No."

"You're sure?"

"I am."

I decided to revisit that question later. "Are you on any medications?"

"Vitamins." She cringed. "Forget I said that."

"What kind of vitamins?"

She gulped. "It's irrelevant."

"Are they a prescription?"

"Let it go, Liam!" She pressed her hands to her mouth, eyes widening. "I'm sorry. I'm just not feeling well."

I suppressed a sigh. "Fine. We'll leave that for now. Are you taking anything else that could affect your blood pressure?"

"No."

"Have you been drinking enough water?"

"Liam." She wiped a hand down her face. "I—"

"I can help you, Ava." I stepped forward, so she could see I meant it. "You just have to be open with me."

True, we had chemistry in spades and I was starting to care for her, but that was not what was going on tonight. I was her doctor here and she needed to trust I'd do what was best for her health.

Her throat bobbed and she gazed up at me with teary eyes. "I don't think I can."

My heart clenched. "Look, if you're ill, it's not your fault. Just let me help you."

Needing to touch her and assure her everything would be fine, I ran a thumb over her cheek. Her eyes fell shut and her face pressed against my hand. I cupped her cheek, wanting to give her comfort.

Her skin was wet and warm, making me frown. No matter how much I wanted to hold her and help her, I couldn't do so until I got to the root of her problem.

"Ava, can you answer me now, truthfully?"

Her chin trembled and she pulled away from my touch.

"Hey, no need to cry. Just tell me what's been going on and I'll—"

"I'm pregnant."

My entire being stilled. I couldn't have heard her right. "What?"

She lifted her face from her behind her hands. "I'm pregnant, Liam."

Oh God.

I took an involuntary step back, shock reeling through me.

"Liam, I—" A sob cut off her words and she continued to cry, her body trembling.

I wasn't sure what to do with myself. My gaze went to the walls, the ceiling, then back to Ava. How did I not realize this?

My head reeled with jumbled thoughts, trying to make sense of it all. Yet the one thing that clutched at my heart the most, that turned my stomach inside out, was one burning question.

I pulled close to Ava in short cautious steps. My heartbeat echoed in my ears and my body was stiff.

But I needed to know. "Ava?"

Her gaze lifted, face splotchy with tears.

I wanted to hold her, tell her everything would be fine. But damn it, I needed to know.

A fresh wave of tears poured down her face and she nodded to the question in my eyes. "It's yours. The baby is yours."

Fuck.

Chapter 17

Ava

I wiped my face and managed to halt the tears. Through the droplets stuck on my lashes, I caught sight of Liam's face. His eyes stared unseeing at the plain wall behind me.

Okay.

I'd never seen him so rattled before. In fact, it wasn't helping my anxiety at all.

The knots in my stomach grew tighter just watching him.

"Liam? Are you okay?"

He blinked, but that was all.

Was he even breathing?

I tilted my head to the side. "Liam?"

A muscle ticked in his jaw and his fingers pressed into a fist—the only signs of life from him.

Shit.

Was he was angry?

I swallowed past the ache in my throat.

This wasn't how this announcement was supposed to

happen. Given the time, I would have prepared better. Maybe start with, "So, funny story…"

My palms grew sweaty and I wiped them down my thighs. "You know what's funny?"

Liam's eyes snapped to my face.

My cheeks heated and now I was speechless. I didn't expect him to respond so quickly. I had no idea what was funny.

Everything was messed up in the most colossal way.

I just needed him to stop looking like he took a slap to the face that had stunned him into silence.

Familiar gray eyes that usually swirled with emotion pinned me with a blank look.

Shit, Ava, what's funny? Think!

"What are the odds, right? I got pregnant after fooling around with one of my dad's friends just once." Hollow laughter escaped from my lips.

It died off when Liam didn't so much as twitch.

I licked my lips, my insides cartwheeling. "It's a crazy story, huh?" I paused. "Not like I was out spreading the news." Lin's face flashed in my head. "Not to anyone who would tell my dad. I'm not that stupid."

Liam's expression had lost some of its edge, awareness returning to his eyes.

"Even if we did tell people, who would believe it? So crazy." I chuckled.

Lines formed between his brows.

I raised my hands. "I'm not telling anyone. Definitely not, but…"

Soon, the tiny curve of my stomach would grow bigger and everyone would know—including my dad.

"It will be alright," I finished in a small voice.

I rested my hand on my belly, comforting myself.

Everything will be alright.

Liam's gaze dropped to my hand and his eyes blinked rapidly as if making a decision. "Let's look at what we're dealing with."

My body stiffened.

I should've been glad he was speaking at all. But his tone was brisk, like I was just another patient. A random stranger who ended up in his clinic by chance.

Not the woman who just told him we were having a baby together.

I sucked in a breath to calm myself. "Yeah, sure."

At least clinical Liam was better than expressionless Liam.

"Lean back."

I flattened my hands on the exam table behind me, leaning back. My shirt drifted up and exposed my midriff.

It was strange being in this position in Liam's clinic, instead of in his bedroom.

His eyes traveled up my body and back down. Normally, his gaze on me would cause heat to pool in my belly. But he wasn't looking at me like that.

His hand slipped into the waistband of my leggings and my breath caught.

I bit my lip, closing my eyes, not sure what to expect.

"These are too tight."

My eyes snapped open.

"You should avoid anything that is constricting." His eyes were fixed on the spot where my waistband met my belly.

"Oh." My face heated. "Okay."

"It could be cutting off your circulation. Inadequate blood flow can cause low blood pressure." He tugged on the waistband, then shimmied it down.

My body relaxed and a sigh escaped my lips. His brow lifted.

He was simply doing his job.

And in an emotionless tone, he went on, "Most people worry about high blood pressure, but having low blood pressure is dangerous, too. Case in point, tonight."

Sheesh. I hugged my arms around myself. I hadn't intended to put myself in this situation.

If Liam saw my discomfort, he made no indication. "To help improve your blood pressure, wear looser clothing."

You said so before.

"Eating frequent meals throughout the day, too, will help. And try not to stand up too fast. Thomas mentioned that earlier."

Like I didn't know that already.

"And don't stay out too long in the sun, or in any hot, humid environment."

That, I didn't know.

"Don't stand on your feet for too long."

Wait, how was that supposed to work? I was almost always on my feet at work.

Dr. Cooper continued, "And drink more water."

"Are you done?"

My snippy tone went right over his head. "Not quite. We need to monitor your blood pressure, but as long as you take care of yourself, you should be fine."

He reached out a hand and my fingers curled in my lap. Now, surely, was when he'd speak about us. But his hand went to my elbow, as if to help me off the exam table.

He was sending me off.

I yanked my arm back. "That's it?"

Liam frowned.

I jumped off the table and landed on my feet. The

solid ground beneath me enforced the emotions rolling through me. All of them morphed into one—anger.

His instructions be damned. Just looking at him cured my low blood pressure. My heart was now hammering away.

"Really? That's it? I just told you we're having a baby and your reaction is to prescribe me a do-and-don't list, then send me on my way?"

His gaze fell. "Ava…"

I pressed closer. "Liam, this is messed up, I know. But I expected some sort of reaction from you. Hell, anything, but this…" I gestured my hands between us, the words dying on my lips. "Don't you have questions? Anything to say? I'm having our baby, for goodness' sake!"

His eyes shot to the door, then back to me. No longer were they blank or indifferently professional. Their gray depths hit me with the force of a tsunami.

I folded my arms across my chest and stood my ground.

"Remember who's in my living room?" He stabbed a finger toward the door. "Your dad. My friend."

"So?"

His eyes bulged. "So, he brought his daughter to me to be treated. His daughter, who he is worried about. His daughter, who I've knocked up."

I pinched the spot between my brows. "Liam, you don't have to—"

"I have to, Ava!" His voice shook. "You're right. This is messed up. But you are wrong about one thing. There's nothing funny about this."

I bit my lip, my anger cooling. An uneasiness grew in my stomach.

His eyes went to the door again and he blew out a

breath. "I'm not going to leave your dad sitting out there any longer than need be."

He murmured something about raising suspicion as he breezed past me.

The door creaked open.

I spun around. "What are you going to tell him?"

Liam stopped in the doorway, his back ramrod straight. "I'll tell him it's your blood pressure."

Relief swooped through me. Not that I expected him to reveal the truth. He didn't seem to have come to terms with it himself.

"I need time."

I looked up.

"This—" his face turned slightly, so I could make out his profile. The muscle in his jaw ticked. "—is a lot."

With that, he walked out. The door swung closed behind him.

I could understand that, I guess. But it was no less disappointing.

But what had I expected him to do? Jump for joy?

I sagged against the exam table. The dizziness was long gone. But a harrowing emptiness took its place.

I doubted drinking water or wearing loose-fitting clothing could fix this.

If I could hide away forever in the sterile exam room, I would. I didn't want to face my dad or Liam or myself. I just wanted to forget my problems.

But Liam was out there, telling Dad half-truths. I needed to play my part. And put up a strong front until we could tell the whole truth.

I pulled in a deep breath.

Just act normal, Ava.

I made my way out of the clinic and down the hall connecting to the house. I was close to the living room when my dad's voice reached me. My feet halted, breath ceasing.

"So, only her blood pressure?"

"Yes."

"I'll encourage her to be more careful." Dad paused. "Nothing like this has ever happened before."

"Illness crops up sometimes without any concrete reason." Liam's voice was surprisingly smooth.

"That it does." Dad groaned and I pictured him stretching. "Like my back has recently started feeling tight. I don't know what's going on."

"It's old age, Thomas."

Dad's laughter boomed. "Thank you, Liam. Excellent diagnosis."

"I know, I'm one of the best."

Since the mood was light, I swallowed my nerves and entered the living room. Dad stopped his teasing and reached for me.

He rubbed my back, his eyes searching my face. "Peanut, how are you feeling?"

I must have scared him earlier. The worry in his gaze clutched at my heart. He deserved to know the truth.

I'd never lied to him and I hated doing so now.

I took a deep breath. "I'm fine, Dad."

"Don't scare me like that again. Do everything Liam suggested, okay?"

My chin trembled. If I uttered another word, I'd surely break into tears. So I settled for a nod and sniff.

"Oh, Peanut." He collected me into his arms.

Warmth cocooned me. I sighed and leaned into my dad. For the first time tonight, everything seemed like it would, indeed, be alright.

He rubbed my back. "Liam took good care of you. You're fine now."

Liam. Worry bolted through me, chasing away the comfort. I blinked open.

Liam hadn't moved from the spot where Dad had left him.

His feet were planted and his arms folded across his chest. The gray depths of his eyes mirrored the orange fire from the fireplace and swirled with an emotion I couldn't name.

The worst part was, the force of it was focused on me.

I stared back at him over Dad's shoulder, unable to look away.

Was he mad at me? Angry about the baby?

Dad pulled away. "Let's get you home, Ava."

He draped an arm across my shoulder and herded us to the door. Liam followed behind.

"You'll email me the bill, right?" Dad paused.

I glanced back and Liam's eyes caught mine, not letting go.

His jaw clenched. "Don't worry about it. It's nothing."

Dad snorted. "I thought you'd say that. I owe you one, regardless."

Liam kept looking at me intently.

"Come on, Peanut."

My eyes broke away from Liam's as we stepped into the night.

"Have a good evening," Dad called back.

Liam didn't respond.

Chapter 18

Liam

I frowned at the notes in my hand. I could have sworn I wrote them down in an earlier file.

Did I mix up the patients' charts?

I picked up the stack I just finished working on and found the records. The initial file belonged to a patient from this morning.

A flip-through proved that, in fact, I did mix up the details.

"Fuck." I slapped the file down.

I covered my face with my hands and groaned. Could today get any worse?

Fixing that confusion would take less than five minutes, but it was a symptom of a much bigger problem. One that had plagued me for the past couple of days. And was only worsening by the minute.

I pulled myself up and stood to look out the window. The sun was high in the afternoon sky and the garden was alive with a gentle breeze playing through it.

This view should give me pleasure. I cherished every moment I could look upon it and be happy about my move back here.

But not today.

My insides felt like I'd swallowed a bunch of needles.

I messed up big time and there was no way around it.

The effect bled into my work. I could hardly keep my head straight. Even though no one else seemed to notice, I knew.

I found myself daydreaming, thinking about Ava. About our child.

My pulse spiked just entertaining the subject.

But worst of all, I had betrayed her father's trust. My best friend.

That felt like I had ten-fold the amount of those needles pricking me.

My appointments usually kept me from lingering over my inner turmoil. But now that my patients had left for the day and the office was quiet, there was no escaping it.

I had a baby on the way—and the mother was my best friend's daughter.

I blew out a breath and dropped back into my chair.

Back to work, Liam.

But try as I might, I couldn't concentrate on more than two lines without my mind wandering. Recalling the hurt look in Ava's eyes. Seeing the trust on her father's face when he looked at me.

I was a terrible friend.

A knock at the door saved me from my thoughts. The receptionist's face poked in.

"Mr. Thomas Morellis is here to see you."

I contemplated saying I wasn't available. Then I mentally kicked myself.

I wasn't a coward.

Steeling myself, I nodded. "Send him in."

Seconds passed before Thomas entered. In addition to khakis and a sweater, he wore a big smile. "Dr. Cooper."

I forced a smile. "Mr. Morellis. Have a seat."

He chuckled and dropped into the visitor's chair. "What's all that?"

"Patient files."

His brows went up, eyes brightening.

I pulled them back, keeping them safely out of his reach. "And you cannot look through them."

"Pfft." He waved a hand and settled back. "I don't need to. I know everything about everyone. No place is as good for gossip as the grocery store aisles."

He knew all but what was right under his nose.

I bit my tongue. That wasn't a topic I was willing to pursue. "Are you here about your back?"

A shadow fell across his face. Odd for a man like Thomas, who had a quick smile for everyone.

"It's about Ava."

A quiver lanced through my stomach. Does he know? Did she tell him?

I doubted Thomas would begin by coming in to sit and talk. Still, I couldn't shake my anxiety.

To hide my shaking hands, I messed with a pen and the files. "What about her?"

It was a small victory my voice came out steady. Dealing with patients taught me to hide my emotions and display calm confidence.

And thankfully, it worked with Thomas.

"She's—" He flattened his hands on the table.

I forced my gaze to meet his.

"Well, I have to thank you for Sunday night, first. She hasn't had an episode like that since."

I nodded, waiting for the inevitable "but."

"She's just not herself, though."

I found myself sitting up. "In what way?"

His eyes wandered, brows pinched like he was trying to picture something I couldn't see.

"She's been a bit distant, you know? I asked if she was still feeling poorly and she says no. When I call her to check in, she always says she's tired and can't talk, or some other excuse." His shoulders made a helpless gesture. "I'm just concerned."

My chest squeezed tight and I fought to pull in a breath. I hadn't reached out to her since Sunday. Now I regretted my hesitation.

I just didn't know what to say or do. It still didn't feel real that we were having a baby. It felt like a dream I would wake up from any moment.

Yet, Ava was already living the reality. Had been for the past few weeks.

If I could make a guess, her new mood had everything to do with me and Sunday night.

But I couldn't go telling Thomas as much. He still looked at me expectantly, waiting for an answer.

I swallowed. "That's curious." Heaven bless the AC for cooling me down now as I perspired under the pressure. "Doesn't sound like a symptom of low blood pressure."

Thomas's frown deepened. "Then what?"

"What if she inhaled too much cleaning product and it's got her lightheaded?" I joked good-naturedly, trying to ease my friend's worry.

Laughter belted from his chest. "Seriously? Well, maybe."

A small smile ticked up my lip, but then I paused.

What if the cleaning products were, indeed, a problem? They might have harsh chemicals that could be harmful to both Ava's and the baby's health.

I needed to check on that as soon as possible. She shouldn't be inhaling anything too strong.

"I'm just worried." Thomas's voice pulled me back to the moment.

"It's possible it has nothing to do with the low blood pressure. She could just be feeling down. She'll come around."

He nodded. "Thank you. Talking with you has helped. I considered camping out on her couch, in case anything else happened."

"I can't imagine that'd go over well with Ava."

"Nah, she'd likely chase me out of the house with a broom."

My laughter caught me off guard.

Thomas grinned. "I'll let her be, since you say not to worry." My friend leaned forward. "I know you refuse payment, but I'd like to do something for you. You've been a great help to us."

"Don't mention—"

"No, really, Liam. Come over for dinner on Sunday."

I had turned down all his invitations since that first night. Finding out Ava was pregnant made me even less inclined to join them.

"I'm busy on Sunday."

"Yeah? I have a second pair of eyes, Liam, I see everything." He held up his glasses.

I shook my head. "That's not how it works."

"I know you must be lonely. You were reading a murder mystery and drinking wine in front of a fireplace all alone the other night."

I pressed my fingers to my forehead. "You weren't supposed to go through my stuff."

"It was out in the open. I merely saw." He tapped his glasses.

"Well, quit looking."

"Can't help it." The smile in his eyes faded to concern. "You don't have to be lonely anymore. Come over on Sundays, okay? You won't be imposing."

He wouldn't say the same once he found out how *not lonely* I'd been with his daughter.

A rebuttal died on my tongue as the phone rang. I snatched up my cell.

An unfamiliar number with no caller ID. Having to choose between answering it and Thomas's badgering, it was an easy choice.

I raised a finger and crossed to the other end of the room.

"This is Dr. Liam Cooper."

"Good afternoon, Dr. Cooper. This is Dr. Morris. There's a patient in my clinic—Miss Ava Morellis."

My heart lurched. I glanced back at Ava's dad, who was looking out the window at my garden.

I swallowed. "Go on."

"She came in for her routine prenatal appointment. But she suddenly broke down." The doctor paused as if turning to look at Ava. "She's panicked and alone. When I asked who I could call for her, she gave me this number. I'm guessing you're someone who can help her."

My chest crowded. *Panicked and alone* echoed in my brain.

Thomas was right. Ava was not alright. And I'd been lost in myself and failed to realize she must be torn up, too.

"I can." I choked out. "I'll be there as soon as possible."

The doctor gave me the address.

It was miles away.

Shit.

I hurried back to my desk.

Thomas promptly turned from the window. "Something wrong?"

I glanced into his worried eyes, my stomach twisting. He was her dad and deserved to know. But now was not the time.

Even though he couldn't be there, I would go to her side.

"A patient needs me." I grabbed two sets of keys and tossed him one. "Lock up the place, okay? Thanks."

Before Thomas could respond, I raced out of the clinic. My hands shook as I opened the car door, got in, and tore down the road.

Despite everything, Ava had reached out to me.

I couldn't keep wallowing. I needed to man up.

I probably broke a few traffic laws, but the sense of urgency increased with every mile that passed. I couldn't delay.

Patients requested my attention all the time. The staff always had questions and updates for me. I had the medical board to report to.

Yet, none of my other responsibilities ever gutted me this way. As though I would crack if I failed to meet and surpass Ava's expectations of me.

It was unbelievable.

I never imagined having a child in my future. I'd dedicated all my time and effort to building a career. It was a foregone conclusion that having a family had passed me by.

Yet, here I was, driving like a maniac to be with the mother of my child.

A feeling sparked in my chest. Warmth and tenderness mixed with worry. For Ava.

For our child.

Who would have thought? Certainly not me.

A hollow laughter tore from my throat.

But it was real now. I was going to be a dad. I'd have a baby that'd grow up into a teenager and then an adult.

I gulped. My own son or daughter.

I never pictured myself as a parent, but I wanted to start now.

I'd do right by them. Give them an honest, good, and simple life.

Support their dreams. Take care of them.

I blinked rapidly and my eyes refocused on the road. For a moment there, I'd been picturing our baby's first steps and graduation hats flying in the air.

It wasn't planned. But it certainly was welcome.

I wanted to be a dad. A damn good one.

And it started now.

I hit the gas pedal, tearing down the road.

Ava needs me. Our child needs me.

Chapter 19

Ava

Nervous energy zinged through my body. I paced to work it off, but it only served to agitate me more. Sweat coated my forehead and my belly tensed.

Ava, you're being ridiculous. The way you freaked out. The doctor will think you're not ready for motherhood. That patient who...

Argh! I pressed my fingernails into my palms. Anything to ground me in the moment and get rid of those negative thoughts.

Nothing had worked in the past hour. And it sure as hell wasn't working now.

What was wrong with me?

I brought my hands to my face and cursed silently into them. How could I fall apart like that?

Dr. Morris must have thought I was unfit having a melt down on her that way.

Crap on a cracker.

My heart rate was spiking again.

Will this never end?

Based on the wall clock, I'd been monopolizing this exam room for far too long. They would surely kick me out soon. Other patients probably had it all together and didn't just lose it when asked about simple things.

Not that simple.

I massaged my temple. Thinking of it all made me want to curl up and cry. The corners of my eyes stung but I sucked in a breath.

I could do this. I could wait for Liam to come.

My cheeks burned and I was glad no one else was here to witness it.

When Dr. Morris asked if she could call someone in to help, I considered Lin. Then quickly squashed the thought.

She was great to cover for me at work and listen when I needed to vent. It wouldn't be fair to demand more of her.

Dad was out of the question. This wasn't the way I wanted him to learn about his grandchild.

That left me with one person.

Liam.

I need time. This is a lot.

My insides turned turbulent. I resumed pacing and watching the clock.

He hadn't reached out to me since Sunday. Was it right to drag him into this? Dr. Morris said he was coming, but would he really?

Was it the type of thing you said to get someone off your back? Or did he really mean it?

Oh God.

If only I wasn't such a mess.

There was no reason to freak out. The meeting had been going well. She asked the typical questions.

How's the baby? How are you doing?

But then she started talking about genetic testing, blood

work, monthly appointments which would become weekly in the final six weeks of the pregnancy, gestational diabetes, and risks such as preeclampsia. I just broke down.

Her question "Do you understand?" was still going off in my head.

I had no reply to that. My heart raced a mile a minute and my brain just shut down.

I hugged my arms around my body, seeking warmth. I shook so badly I couldn't stay still.

All of this was too much. I couldn't do it all on my own. I needed support. I needed Liam.

Tears formed in my eyes but I blinked them away.

He was coming, right?

I didn't dare call him. What if he turned me down? That might hurt worse than not seeing or hearing from him at all.

I hoped like hell he'd show up.

Hannibal was a long drive away. And he worked, too.

Oh my goodness, I had dragged him away from his job. His patients.

I'm such a terrible person!

Voices sounded outside the door. I spun to it. Surely, they'd come to kick me out.

Liam wasn't coming and I was taking up space.

I reached for my purse so I could leave as soon as they came in. No need to drag out the inevitable.

The door swung open, but it wasn't a security team here to kick out the ridiculous patient.

I blinked, disbelief tugging at my insides.

My mouth parted. "Liam?"

His usually styled-to-perfection hair was windblown and disheveled. He didn't have on a jacket. The sleeves of his button-down bunched around his elbows and the open top button exposed his chest.

All of this worried me. He looked like he'd raced over here. But it was his gray eyes, settling on mine and flooding with relief that clutched at my heart.

"This is Dr. Liam Cooper whom you asked for, is it not?" Dr. Morris took a step into the room, looking between us.

I found the strength to nod.

"Good." Still giving us a look, she said, "I'll see to another patient while you two talk."

She inclined her head slightly before leaving. The door clipped shut, leaving us alone together.

Liam jerked into motion. He rushed over to me, his arms open and inviting.

All the tension in my gut melted, and my body turned weak. Just in time as his arms wrapped around me. He pulled me against his hard chest, cocooning my body.

I tucked my head at the base of his throat and drew in deep breaths. All of him, his warmth, his cologne.

I flattened my palms on his chest, feeling his strength beneath my fingers. "You're here," I whispered.

"I'm here, princess." His throat bobbed with a rough swallow.

Tears welled up in my eyes. This time, I was powerless to stop them. The first drop touched my cheek.

"I was so scared. I—"

"Shh," he cooed, stroking my hair. "It's okay, Ava."

His calm voice combined with the soothing touch only made my tears fall harder.

"Ava…" He squeezed me some more. "It will be alright."

My tears soaked through his shirt but he only held me closer. How was he being so understanding?

I slipped my hands down and wrapped them around

him, pinning my body to his. He felt like home and comfort, and I just needed both so badly.

"I was... I didn't mean to break down," I sobbed.

He didn't stop, just continued to trace his palm down my back and run his fingers through my hair.

"I thought I could handle it all. I just didn't think—" I drew back to look at his face. "I'm sorry, Liam."

I was pretty sure my nose was wet and red and my face splotchy. But Liam's gaze held only warmth and acceptance.

"You have nothing to apologize for, Ava."

"But I do." The last word was drawn out as fresh tears ran down my face.

I buried my cheek against his chest once more. "I'm sorry for all of it. The way you found out, lying to my dad, pulling you away from your work today... I thought I could handle it alone. But then I came here and Dr. Morris started talking about genetic testing and preeclampsia and diabetes—" *hiccup* "—I don't want anything to happen to the baby. I don't want my feet to get swollen. I just want everything to be fine."

"It will be."

I drew back. "How? You don't know that." I wiped the tears from my blurry eyes. "Wait, you do, because you're a doctor. But you don't know for sure!"

"Come here." Liam's voice was slightly amused as he pulled me back against him.

I sagged against him, my sobs turning into tears, and then into shudders.

"It's going to be okay, Ava," he whispered against my ear.

A shiver racked through my body and I pressed closer. Somehow, everything he said in his smooth, calm voice sounded true and assuring to my worried mind.

"I've got you." He cemented that with a quick kiss on my temple.

My eyes, impossibly, got wet once more. I sniffed and hugged him tighter.

"You're not alone in this. I'm going to be here with you for every appointment, okay?"

"You-you are?"

"Yes, and you won't have to deal with everything on your own. We'll do it together."

"But you already know everything."

He chuckled softly. "Well, then, I'll help you understand the steps and keep you informed so you can make confident decisions."

I released a sigh. "You will?"

"Yes, sweetheart." He pulled back and looked into my eyes.

I clenched my teeth to stop my chin's wobbling, but it was futile. I was a mess.

Liam captured my jaw with his thumb and index finger and dropped a kiss on my forehead. "We've got this."

We.

I swallowed, allowing the sensation to wash over me. "Liam?"

His brow rose, waiting.

"I hope you're not saying this because—" My eyes dropped from his to the map my tears drew on his chest. "Well, because you pity me. You said you needed time and I made you come all the way out here. Do you really want to be here, or—"

"Ava," his voice was warm, but gently chiding.

My gaze went back to his.

"I'm here because I want to be. I'm only mad at myself because it took me so long to see what was right in front of me this entire time."

My ribs expanded to contain my rapidly beating heart. What did that mean? Were we still talking about babies and appointments, or something more?

"Look." Liam cupped my cheeks with both hands. "All of this will work out, okay?"

My lips mouthed the word before my mind caught up. *Okay.*

"We're in this together."

I nodded. "Okay."

A smile stretched across his face and I found myself smiling back.

Now that the crying was over, Liam didn't pull away. He seemed eager to remain close. I had zero problems with that.

"We're having a baby," I whispered.

His smile shone brighter. "We are."

I chuckled at the surprised look on his face. For the first time since all of this started, true excitement started to work its way through me.

I had Liam's support. And enthusiasm, if the light in his eyes was anything to go by.

"Are we ready to see the doctor?" He searched my face.

"Sure." I took a step back and ran my fingers through my hair.

Then I caught his shirt.

"Oh, I messed up your..." I waved my hand at his chest.

Liam looked down and patted the area carelessly. "It's nothing."

His eyes stayed on me, though. Like I was his main priority here.

Warmth fluttered through me. He had dropped everything to be here. On short notice.

My hands suddenly shook for a different reason. I

tucked a lock of hair behind my ear. "I think I'll go get the—"

The door opened and Dr. Morris walked in. She looked between both of us and her eyes warmed.

"Okay, Mom and Dad, let's try this again, shall we?"

My brows furrowed. How did she know?

"Dr. Cooper told me when he got here," she supplied.

My cheeks heated. "Of course."

Both doctors laughed, like there was a joke I wasn't in on. Thank heavens, for their sake, I was in a better mood, so I smiled.

Dr. Morris asked if I was okay before she resumed our earlier conversation.

Liam's fingers interlaced with mine and his warmth pressed close to me. Half of what she said sounded like a foreign language, but at least I wasn't freaking out this time.

He was here. I wasn't alone.

We've got this.

Chapter 20

Liam

"Hey, what about that one?" Ava pointed to a quaint little restaurant tucked between two towering buildings.

"Sure." I placed a hand on her back as we crossed the road.

She walked in a near skip, her brown hair bouncing around her face. We'd just hit the sidewalk when she turned a full smile on me.

"This is so cool. I've never stopped by for lunch the other times I've come here."

Late lunch, to be exact. The sun swept low in the sky and the temperature was cooler.

"Time to try something new, right?"

She beamed. "Come on."

Ava took my hand and led the way into the restaurant. It housed only a few tables. But a couple were empty.

As a couple, we claimed the one closest to the window.

Ava sighed as she sat. Then she looked out the window with wide brown dreamy eyes.

Thinking about the first time I saw her today and now, she was a completely different woman. Her mood lifted quickly after I assured her I was going to be there for her throughout the pregnancy.

It also helped that Dr. Morris was kind and generous with the compliments. *You're doing great, Ava. For a first-time mom, you're getting this pretty quickly.*

And Ava would blush, happy to with the compliments.

If Dr. Morris was a man, I would be jealous. As it was, I planned to give her some attention of my own when we found the time. She needed to know I would always take care of her—in more ways than one.

But for now, I enjoyed this happy version of Ava.

"What are we having?" Ava scanned the menu. She worried her lip between her teeth, eyes flicking over it. "I don't want to overeat. I'll get queasy on the drive back."

I looked at my menu. The array of choices couldn't hold my attention for more than a second. My eyes kept returning to Ava.

"I'll have the roasted chicken, mashed potatoes, and a milkshake." She leaned forward, her breasts plumping on her folded arms, rising out of her top enticingly. "What are you having?"

It took a few seconds to force my gaze back up. Just then, the waiter appeared and asked the same question. After Ava answered, both women turned to me.

"I'll have what she's having."

The waiter left and Ava rewarded my presence with a sweet smile.

"What's on your mind?"

You. "I'd say the doctor's appointment went well, right?"

"Yes! Oh, gosh. I thought it'd be a mess the way it started. But it's all good now." She was nearly hopping in

her seat. "I had no idea everything was pretty straightforward. It was terrifying at first. And I don't mind all the tests
now."

A chuckle worked up my throat. "Yes, that's good."

"Oh, and my blood pressure is stable." She reached
over and touched my arm. "Can you believe it?"

My lips stretched in a smile. "Yes, it's amazing."

"I can't wait to see our tiny baby on the ultrasound and
hear the baby's heartbeat."

I kept from mentioning that this early, what would
show up would look nothing like a fully developed baby.
Her smile was too precious to ruin. "Dr. Morris said next
month."

"Ugh, next month is too far away. I want to do everything right now."

"What about we take it slow?" I collected her hand in
mine. "Alright?"

She rolled her eyes playfully. "Alright." Then her gaze
slanted at me. "How come you're this calm?"

I wasn't. My heart felt like it was bubbling over. And
every time Ava spoke, the feeling grew bigger.

Daring me to try to contain it.

I was like a kid at Christmas with presents spread out
under the tree. Except now, my present was Ava and she
was carrying the most precious bundle in the universe.

"I'm not, really. But I'm very happy."

She eyed me. "Dr. Cooper, you're a mystery."

My lip ticked up. And Ava answered with a ear-to-ear
full-on grin.

As if tired, she exhaled and dropped back into her seat.
A lingering smile played on her lips. "It's all because you
came."

"What is?"

"How well the appointment went. Thank you for being

there, Liam."

My throat closed up. Why did she sound like I was doing her a favor? "There was nowhere else I'd rather be, Ava. Thank you for calling me."

Our gazes held for a few seconds. Before I could decipher what passed between us, the waiter returned with our orders.

Ava's eyes twinkled as she took in the meal. I frowned. When had she last eaten?

I kept that thought locked up, though. She'd had enough doctoring for one day.

She moaned around a mouthful of potatoes and licked her full pink lips.

I tore my gaze away and focused on filling my empty stomach.

"How is this going to work?"

I lifted my gaze. A line formed between Ava's brows. I wanted it gone immediately and replaced by one of her big smiles.

"How what's going to work?"

She gestured between us. "Being a mom and dad?" Her nose wrinkled.

I felt it in my chest, too. It was weird thinking of us that way. But pleasant, too.

I thought about her question. "We're both in Hannibal. It shouldn't be a problem."

"Yeah, well. I didn't know what your schedule was like today, and I called you away from your patients."

"I can take time off. I own the clinic."

She pursed her lips. "Are you always this cocky?"

"Yes. You never noticed before?"

"Mm-hmm." She picked up her glass and pulled a drink from the straw.

Our eyes met and Ava rolled her tongue around it.

My cock jerked in my pants. "Ava."

She giggled and put the drink down. Her smile withered almost immediately. "But think about it, Liam. How will we manage? You may not have been busy today, but another day, you might be."

"Ava…"

"And we're different people, too. You're a sophisticated doctor from New York and I'm Ava, the house cleaner. Those are worlds apart! How will——"

"Hey." I took her hand in mine, rubbing it softly. "We'll make it work. People make crazy situations work all the time. Don't get all worked up, okay?"

She bit her lip. "You're sure?"

I nodded. "100 percent." I frowned. "Well, more like ninety-nine, since there's the 1 percent that is Thomas."

"Oh, crap. My dad." Ava pulled her hand from mine to curl it in her lap. "He's a huge 1 percent."

She probably was twisting her fingers into a pretzel with worry. If I could, I'd say something reassuring. But nothing came to mind.

Between the both of us, we would work things out. Thomas was another challenge all on its own.

We stayed silent for a few moments before Ava broke it.

"I don't like lying to him." Her eyes were hidden from me as she looked down at her lap. "I've always told him everything. He's been all I've had my whole life. I feel lousy keeping this from him."

"Ava, look at me."

Her head came up and the torn look in her eyes razored through me.

"It's not real until Dad knows." Her lips trembled. "I don't want to disappoint him." A pause, then her brows shot up. "Wait, no. That didn't come out right. I'm not saying sleeping with you at all is a cause for someone to feel disappointed. Or having a baby with you is wrong, it's just—"

She was red in the face. I could let this go on. The beginnings of a smile were already pulling at my lips. I bit on my inner cheek to hide it.

"I get it."

"Oh, um, thanks." She offered me a small smile. "What are we going to do, Liam?"

I exhaled, looking out at the fading sun. Thomas had been my friend forever. The last thing I wanted was for him to feel betrayed.

Or think I took advantage of our closeness to get to Ava. Or worse, that I preyed on her.

I knew Thomas too well. That's exactly where his mind would go. There was no helping it.

I feared the fallout. Especially for Ava's sake. He loved and doted on her. I didn't want to ruin their relationship.

Or our friendship.

My shoulders hunched at the thought.

"Liam?" Ava's soft voice brought me back to the present.

I turned to her wide-eyed brown gaze. I swallowed the lump in my throat. She trusted me to be here, to help.

Not spiral into worst-case-scenario thoughts.

But I couldn't lie, either.

"Thomas probably won't take it well."

She sighed like I confirmed what she thought.

"He may feel betrayed, angry…"

"Disappointed."

"But we can't control how he feels, Ava. We can't control how anyone feels."

Her eyes fell shut and she muttered, "I know. I'm just— I don't want anything to go wrong. Can't he just be happy for us?"

I scoffed. "I doubt that."

"So, what do we do?"

Our gazes held and I knew she was thinking what I was thinking. But neither of us was inclined to say it first. When it was finally out in the open, there would be no taking it back and we'd have to follow through.

"Tell him," Ava stated firmly.

"Tell him," I echoed at the same time.

"Aw, shit." Ava slumped in her seat. "I was hoping you'd say 'run away.'"

I chuckled. "I'm too old to run."

Her gaze roamed hungrily up my body, contradicting my statement. But she didn't comment. "And I'll be too big to run in a few months."

She rubbed her belly.

A couple of seconds passed.

"So, we're telling him."

I leaned forward and held my left hand out. She placed her right one in mine. "Are you okay with that?"

She squeezed my hand and nodded. "Yes."

"Good."

"When?"

"He invited me over for dinner on Sunday."

"This Sunday?" Her chest started to rise and fall under her pale pink blouse.

I nodded and firmed my hold on her hand. "The sooner the better, don't you think?"

She swallowed. "I guess."

"If we don't do this, we'll never stop looking over our shoulders."

"I'm not ready."

"Well, there are four days to get ready."

Ava eyed me. "You're way too calm."

I smiled. "I'm not."

She smiled back.

"What if we put that on a back burner for now? We're miles away from Hannibal and it's a lovely evening. No need to worry ourselves sick tonight."

She smiled and extracted her hand, resuming her eating. "Okay." Her eyes went to my plate. "Let's play a game. First to finish eating wins."

I chuckled. "And what's the prize?"

"The winner gets the other person's leftovers."

"Wait, you said you'd feel queasy if you ate too much."

"I'm having a good day." She tapped her stomach. "Are you scared? Trying to wiggle your way out?"

I raised a brow.

She was already halfway done. But I was also very competitive.

"Let's do it."

"Okay, ready?"

I nodded.

We dug in.

"Oh my God, Liam! You're going too fast. Go back to picking at your food."

"It's a competition! What am I supposed to do?" I mumbled around a mouthful.

"But your mouth's bigger than mine."

"How?"

"It is!"

I resumed shoveling chicken into my mouth. "I won't go easy on you."

"That's it!" She threw herself into it, not looking at me.

Smiling, I sat back and watched her. She could have my plate and five more. Whatever she wanted.

As long as the fire in her eyes kept blazing and her sweet smile remained.

Chapter 21

Ava

Darkness surrounded the truck and bled into its interior. I turned sideways to look at Liam, but the shadows hid his face. I couldn't make out his emotions.

Aside from the tires rolling on the highway and the engine's rumbling, everything else was silent.

And I was feeling bold.

I leaned over the center console and dragged a hand up his thigh.

"Thought you were tired." He side-eyed me.

"Not anymore." I let my fingers trail upward to his zipper.

Liam hissed a harsh breath. "Ava, you're going to make us crash."

I gave him one last brush before removing my hand. "No we won't. I'm confident of your driving skills."

He loosened his grip on the wheel. "Don't tempt fate."

"Fate would cooperate better than you," I pouted.

"You're trouble, Ava."

I smiled and sent my eyes downward. Just a brush and his shaft was already growing thick. If I tried again, I was certain he would be more willing.

"Don't you dare."

It was as if he'd read my mind.

My gaze trailed up to his unbuttoned shirt, his strong masculine throat, and his face. A car zoomed past, lighting up his eyes for a second.

The dark warning in them set my blood on fire.

"Okay." My lip quirked. "I won't."

He huffed a disbelieving sound.

I smiled and settled back in my seat.

It was so dark out I hardly saw beyond the scope of the headlights. I craned my neck. Twinkling stars spread across the sky, but no moon.

"I could have driven myself, you know."

"It's too dark and too late. I don't want you on the road by yourself," Liam clipped out.

I blew out a breath. "So what am I to do tomorrow? Walk around Hannibal?"

"I'll take you wherever you need to go." He paused. "And I'll get someone to drive your car back to Hannibal. You'll have it back by evening."

I rolled my eyes but kept my thoughts to myself.

"We shouldn't have stayed out so late," Liam muttered.

Eating all my dinner plus Liam's remaining dinner didn't sit in my stomach so well. It was fun to win, though. So after our late lunch, we took a walk around town.

It was a beautiful, peaceful place. Not so unlike Hannibal. Only there, we didn't know anyone.

Liam laced his fingers with mine and dropped occasional kisses on my temple. He seemed to do so without thinking. But each sign of affection sent my pulse racing.

Too bad we had to leave. Now, he was getting back to his usual stoic self.

"I miss it already."

Liam turned to me, his jaw softening. He placed a hand on my thigh and rubbed gently. "Maybe next time we'll stay longer."

"Okay."

While his left hand navigated the wheel, his right hand remained on my lap. The small taps were for comfort, but my body yearned for a different kind of petting.

Biting my lip, I worked my dress up. Just a little. So I could feel the brush of his palm against my skin.

Liam started to turn.

"It's quiet on the road tonight."

"Yeah, it's different from the afternoon. I've never driven this route before."

He was distracted.

Yes! Just keep him talking.

"Me too." I adjusted in my seat and my dress rode up. His hand grazed my bare skin and I bit back a moan. "Well, the first day I saw Dr. Morris was my first time driving it, too."

"How many appointments did you have with her?"

"Just a few."

He absentmindedly rubbed my thigh.

Oh, fuck.

I dropped lower in the seat and his hand inched up. My eyes rolled back in my head.

If I had driven myself, I'd have missed this.

"Ava."

The rough sound of Liam's voice forced my eyes open. His gaze was heavy with disapproval.

A few seconds ago, I would have stopped and laughed

it off. But my nipples strained against my lace bra and my panties grew more damp as each second passed.

Despite his annoyance, his hand still rested in the same spot. Shaking just a bit. Eager to touch me, but holding back?

Well, no more.

I tilted my hips and directed his hand to where I needed it. He cupped my mound and I moaned. I bit my lip, angling to get more.

"We shouldn't be doing this."

But he stroked my clit through my panties, his breathing getting heavier.

"Yes, right there." My pussy was wet now. "Right. There."

Suddenly, his hand disappeared.

My eyes snapped open.

He was back to clutching the steering wheel with both hands. "It's late. We should get home."

Ugh, fine.

On second thought… "Whatever you say, daddy."

He slanted a dark look at me and I smiled. Raising a brow, I dipped my hand underneath my dress.

I planned to taunt him but need sparked through my body. My body curved and I moaned as I rubbed my clit.

Liam's murmured curse only spurred me on. I wasn't acting anymore. My fingers flew as I reached for the delicious peak.

All the sensations heightened with the knowledge that Liam watched. I licked my lips. He'd see me come and regret not letting go of his rigid composure.

The truck swerved to the side and lurched to a stop.

Before I could grasp what was happening, Liam got out. He stalked over to my side and threw the door open.

He lifted me out of my seat and deposited me on the ground. "Spread your legs."

Small stones bit into my bare soles but I was too needy to mind. I pushed my knees apart, my chest rising and falling rapidly.

Liam dropped to the ground before me and reached under my dress. Firm fingers brushed my skin before latching onto my panties and tearing them off.

His head disappeared and not a second later, a firm lick ran up my center.

A gasp left me. My knees buckled but his hands caught the backs of my thighs and pinned me against the car.

A groan came from underneath my dress as Liam rolled his tongue around my clit. His hands climbed higher, massaging my ass.

My face was to the sky and my cry eclipsed the chirping crickets. This was so scandalous but there was nothing but empty roads around us.

And even if a car were to pass by now, I doubted I'd feel any shame. The only thing I could feel was the pleasure Liam gave me.

I lived for it.

He dipped his tongue into my core and I cried out. I caught my dress and pulled it up, eager to see.

It was dark but the proximity was close enough to make Liam out. His tongue lapped at my folds and his gray eyes were bright with lust, holding my gaze.

My eyes slid lower to his left hand wrapped around his cock through his pants, stroking.

All of it combined with his relentless attention on my center shot pleasure up my spine.

I grabbed onto his shoulders, rolling my hips into his face.

His groan was ragged. "That's it, princess. Get your juices all over daddy's face."

My channel clenched at that moment and my release knocked the strength out of my body. Liam grabbed both of my legs to hold me up while he licked until the tremors stopped.

Next thing I knew, the back passenger door opened and Liam nudged me to sit.

"Is this is what you wanted?" His voice was rough. "Fucking in the middle of nowhere?"

"I was just—"

"No, princess. You've been a bad girl, tempting me all evening."

My heart raced so fast I could hear my breath sawing out of my lungs. I blinked against the darkness. What was he waiting for?

Liam was tugging furiously at his belt buckle.

My mouth watered instantly and I raised shaky hands to help. The zipper parted and I swallowed.

Liam hissed as my searching fingers closed around his heated length.

He closed his hand around the base and fisted his cock. "Do you want to suck daddy's cock?"

I didn't need to be asked twice.

I ran my tongue over the plump head, licking up every drop of precum. Then rounded my lips and took him into my mouth.

Liam's guttural groan filled the night. "Fuck, Ava."

He braced both hands on my head, coaxing gently.

"Take my cock, princess. Be a good girl and do as you're told."

Lust replaced the blood in my veins. I pressed forward and took all of him until I could hardly breathe. Like I had something to prove.

Then I pulled away with a gasp and did it all again.

Liam grunted, encouraging me with quick flexes of his hips.

My core wept, wanting to replace my mouth. But I needed to prove to Liam I was a good girl.

I pulled back and whispered, "Am I doing it right, daddy?"

"Yes, sweet Ava. Just how I like it." He pushed himself between my lips and rolled his hips.

We both moaned.

I couldn't take it anymore. I pulled my mouth off him with a pop and he stepped back.

His brows knotted, a question in his eyes.

"I want you inside me."

"Of course, baby girl. Get on your hands and knees."

Even before the last word fell from his lips, I was moving into position. My knees braced on the seat with my ass in the air. All for his pleasure.

Liam gave an appreciative growl and caressed my backside, chasing off the chill. I felt a soft kiss on my lower back, right before I felt him fill me.

"Oh, Liam."

"Yes, princess," he whispered in my ear, then dropped a kiss on my shoulder. "Is this what you wanted?"

He thrust deep and my back arched.

"Y-yes."

"Fucking out in the open?"

Thrust.

He curled a fist around my hair and pulled. "Hmm?"

My knees buckled.

Liam caught on quickly and wrapped a hand around my waist to steady me. But then his fingers drifted down and ran over my clit.

A cry escaped me, shivers running through my limbs.

"So wet—" he circled my clit "—so eager."

"Liam—"

"Want to come for me, Ava? Want to milk my cock?" he rasped, his thrusts quickening.

"Yes!"

The slap of our bodies echoed in the dark and carried into the cool night.

"Want all my cum? Want it to run down your thighs?" He pressed down on me, his finger working faster.

"Oh, Liam."

"Call me daddy."

My cry rent the air.

Something about his deep, throaty voice saying that had my legs shaking, my body pushing back to meet his. "Oh, God—daddy, I'm going to come."

"It's okay, princess. Do it. Come all over my cock."

I cried out as my core clenched around him. Pleasure bolted through me. My moans carried into the night.

We were out in the middle of nowhere. Who knew who —or what—could be hearing us? But I couldn't bring myself to care.

Only feel.

And it felt so goddamn good.

Liam's body stiffened above me and he came with a roar. Warmth flooded me and spilled down my thighs.

"So good, Ava." He kissed my neck, thrusting one more time. "Such a good girl."

I sighed and sagged against the seat. Shivers still raced through me, but Liam covered me, keeping me warm.

"Can't believe I'll still need to drive to Hannibal after this," Liam huffed.

I giggled. "I can help."

"Not on your life."

I rolled my eyes. "You're overprotective."

"Am I? Really?" He stroked his semi-hard cock in and out of me.

"Liam!"

"What did you say?"

"Nothing. I'm sorry, okay?"

"You better be." He smacked my ass playfully. "Let's get dressed. We still have a ways to go."

I whimpered as his cock left me.

"When we get back, alright?"

I grinned against the seat. He knew me too well. "Okay."

Chapter 22

Liam

Ava led the way into her apartment and flipped on the light switch. A warm glow enveloped the living room. Everything was in its place, neat and organized.

Until she shucked off her shoes and tossed her scarf on a chair. Then she raised both arms and yawned.

"You need to go to bed."

I shouldn't have let us walk the streets for so long. She seemed okay in the moment. But it likely was too much.

Plus, having crazy hot sex on the way home didn't help.

"It's not even that late. I told you I'm fine."

"You're tired, so the time makes little difference." I moved to her and ran a thumb over her cheek. "You'll get some sleep?"

"Yes, I guess so." She turned her back to me.

It took a few seconds to catch on, but then I did and drew her zipper down.

"Need anything else?" I kissed the soft curve of her neck.

She moaned softly, tilting her head for more.

I wrapped an arm around her waist and drew her up against me. Her sweet feminine fragrance and the brush of her hair against my cheek spurred me on. Then the little kisses turned into sucking and I growled low in my throat.

Ava spun in my arms and pressed her soft lips to mine. Her hands rode up my chest and went to my hair, rubbing my scalp.

What was I doing? She needed sleep.

"Ava," I rasped, capturing her hands in mine and pulling them away. "We shouldn't."

"But we could," she whispered.

The sound went straight to my cock. I contemplated giving in for one second but shook off the thought.

"It's been a long day. You're tired."

"Not anymore." Her eyes twinkled and she reached for my buttons.

"Ava." I caught her hands between mine.

If she touched me again, I'd forget myself and that wouldn't be good for her.

She blew out a breath. "Okay."

"Hang on, you have that look."

"What look?" She raised both brows over wide, inno-cent brown eyes.

"That look that says you're just agreeing with me until I let my guard down again."

We were both thinking of the drive home. I could see it by the blush on her cheeks and her eyes dropping from mine.

"That's not what I'm doing."

"If you say so."

"It's not!"

"Prove it."

Her eyes shot to mine. "Fine. I will."

"Okay."

She huffed and spun on her heel, headed to the bedroom.

I chuckled. That should turn her off for a while.

When she came back out, I'd leave so she'd get some rest.

Then I remembered.

"Ava?"

"Yes?" Her voice came out muffled from the bedroom.

"Where are the cleaning products you use for your business?"

It took a few seconds for her to answer. Probably wondering why I asked.

"In the cabinet under the sink."

I took off my shoes and went in search of the products.

I was crouched by the cabinet, reading the labels on the bottles when Ava came back out.

"What are you doing?"

I glanced up. She was in a bright purple nightshirt that clung to her frame and highlighted her curves.

The temptation to say nothing and instead collect her in my arms and kiss her silky lips was too strong.

I pulled my gaze back to the bottle. "Just making sure everything you use is free of harmful chemicals."

"Why?" She leaned against the counter, looking down.

"You're pregnant. And these are all organic. Safe for pregnant women."

"Oh my gosh, seriously?" A rueful smile pulled at her cheeks.

"Yes." I put the products back and shut the cabinet.

"So, is that all, Dr. Cooper?"

I ignored her teasing tone and rose to my feet. "No, you have to be careful, too."

"In what way?" She folded her arms across her chest, watching me.

"The positions you take."

"Oh, like this one?" She flattened both hands on the counter and stuck her ass out.

"Ava…"

She wiggled her pert backside, tempting me to no end.

"I'm serious."

"Okay." She giggled, straightening. "What positions?"

Now that she'd put the idea in my head, it was hard to get out. But I managed.

"Can you avoid certain tasks?"

"Like what?" A line formed between her brows.

She loved what she did and I wasn't about to veto everything.

"Like cleaning the bathtub. You'd have to bend over and—"

"Isn't the baby protected in the womb and secure in my body? And right now, they're very, very tiny."

I paused. Good point.

"But bending over like that engages the abdominals in a way that's not completely safe for you and the baby, especially doing it as often as you're required."

"Oh yeah?" She pulled close and ran a finger down my chest. "I recall bending over just a couple of hours ago and it wasn't a problem then."

"Yeah, that." I bowed my head, a flush running up my neck. "I wasn't thinking."

"I like you when you're not thinking."

I lifted my gaze to meet hers. Her eyes gleamed suggestively.

"Remember our bet?"

She bit her lip, eyes rolling up. "Yes. Is my time up yet?"

"Not quite. But soon."

"I don't like this bet."

"I know." I ran my hands down her sides to her hips and back up to her trim waist. "You have to be careful, Ava."

"I am careful."

"No backbreaking positions, no strenuous activities, none of that."

"Okay."

"And anytime you feel even a bit uncomfortable, take a break immediately."

She laughed. "Liam, you worry too much."

"I'm worried just the right amount." I nuzzled her cheek. "It's my baby in there and I need to make sure you're both safe and healthy."

"Liam…" Her face turned a pretty pink, her eyes soft. "That's sweet."

I smiled and pulled her securely against me. She fit just right. Like we were made for each other.

The words danced on my tongue but I swallowed them. We'd been through enough today, and I didn't want to rock the boat and cause her any more strain.

Would it scare Ava off if I said something like that?

The question evaporated from my mind as her lips met mine. Soft and sweet and searching. She tasted like mint toothpaste and home.

Her soft moans played on my senses, and reeled me in, drugging me.

I lifted her up and placed her on the counter, just to get her off her feet.

She spread her thighs and pulled me close. Her tender hands ran through my hair, down my face, and landed on my chest. Like she couldn't get enough.

Neither could I.

My cock turned to steel in my pants but the last thing I wanted was for this to go further.

It was oddly comforting to just hold her, and feel her in my arms. With her lips playing across mine and our tongues tangling.

"Oof!"

I pulled away, a bit breathless. "Ava, are you okay?" I searched her face.

"No, not really." She pressed a hand to her stomach.

"Was it a cramp?" My mind worked with all the reasons why she could be hurting.

"Kinda."

I frowned.

"I think I'm hungry again."

"God, Ava." I sighed and rested my head against her shoulder. "Way to scare a man."

"What?" She rubbed my back, then my shoulders. "I'm really hungry."

"Fine, we'll get you something. What do you want?"

"Pizza with pineapple on top."

"What?" I reared back. "Really?"

"Yeah, I don't know. I'm just craving it badly."

I chuckled. "Okay, we'll get you…pizza with pineapple." It was a struggle to repress my shudder.

"Kiss me before it gets here because you look like you won't after I eat something like that."

"What? No…"

Ava's eyes remained narrowed.

"Okay, okay, come here."

She laughed and pulled me back in. After a few seconds, she broke off. "That pizza, though."

"I'm on it."

I helped her off the counter. While she went back to the living room, I called in the order.

"What are we watching?" I dropped onto the couch.

Ava scooted closer and tucked herself in the crook of my arm. Her softness, warmth, and sweet smell went to my head. I didn't hear her answer.

All I could focus on was wrapping my arm around her shoulder, keeping her secure against me. She belonged here.

"Have you seen it before?"

"No." I never watched TV.

"Oh, this will be fun."

Ava's eyes stayed glued to it, a small smile on her lips. Watching the light play on her features was more enjoyable for me. But I managed to tear my eyes away for a few moments to catch the show.

It was a home makeover. Every few scenes, Ava would rant about what they were doing. I had no idea what any of it meant, but it was important to her, so I paid attention enough to get the gist of it.

"Is she changing the kitchen floors to hardwood?"

"She's not supposed to do that! It'll be a disaster." Ava looked aghast.

"Crazy Teresa."

"And Jan said not to. Why didn't she listen to him?"

"It's probably a power play."

"Right? She wants to seem important and make the decisions. Ends up making the wrong ones!"

The pizza arrived just as the show's host presented the renovated home to the family. After I collected the boxes and came back, the scene was somber-looking.

"What did I miss?"

"They hated the makeover."

"Oh, that's too bad." I reclaimed my spot and opened Ava's pizza box.

She dove in immediately, still commiserating with the homeowners.

I flipped my pizza box open and she scooted closer.

"What did you get? Oh, extra cheese." Her eyes rounded.

"You want some?"

A smile curved her lips. "Would that be greedy? I keep eating your food."

"I don't mind." She looked unconvinced. "Fine, we'll swap slices."

Two slices in and Ava wasn't going for the pizza anymore. She leaned against me, her head on my chest.

"So cool they redid Teresa's bad designs."

"Will she be kicked off the show?"

"Nah, the drama is good for ratings."

"Hmm, makes sense."

I rubbed her arm, watching the homeowners' six months update. They loved their new house and took good care of it.

Speaking of homes, I looked around Ava's. It was cozy and warm. Full of plants.

Nice for a single woman. But not much space for a baby to move around without obstacles.

"Hey, do you think—"

A sharp inhale cut me off.

"Ava?" I brushed her hair to the side.

Her eyes were closed and she was fast asleep.

I eased her down onto my lap and she stretched her feet. But not once did her eyes open.

She must have been very tired.

I rubbed her back, encouraging her rest. She needed the strength for herself and the baby.

I wanted the best for them both.

They were quickly becoming all I cared about it. I'd

been back in Hannibal for a couple of hours and hadn't reached out to Thomas about the locking up at the clinic. I'd do so tomorrow.

For now, Ava was all I could think of.

Was living here the best for her and the baby? It seemed too small. Plus, I'd like to be around for night feedings and all the chaos that came with a newborn.

We couldn't do that here.

When the time was right, I'd ask her to move in with me. The decision settled in my chest.

I ran my hands through the silky strands of her hair.

Would she like that? My pulse was already racing just thinking of it. Even before I considered all the angles, it was clear what I felt in my heart.

No more quiet, boring nights alone. No more Ava rushing to leave the next morning. We would be together.

But first, we needed to tell Thomas.

Chapter 23

Ava

A knock rattled the front door, prodding me off the couch. Who the heck was that? It came again.

I frowned. Was I expecting someone?

Oh, right. Liam. Dinner with my dad.

I rubbed my racing heart and went to the door. My hand slipped on the handle so I wiped it on my dress and tried again. This time, it worked.

"Hey."

Liam was in a silk black shirt tucked into black dress pants and shiny black dress shoes. His face was clean-shaven and his hair was styled to perfection, as usual.

Despite looking like a dream come to life, the butterflies in my stomach weren't for him.

"Ava?" His eyebrows pulled together. "Are you okay?"

"Mm-hmm. I'm excellent." I back walked into the living room. "H-how are you? You good?"

He followed me inside and closed the door. The frown never left his face. "You sure?"

"Can't you tell? It's a beautiful day. I've never been this good."

His face crumpled, sympathy lining his eyes. "Worried?"

I swallowed, my fake bravado falling apart. "Can't we just say something came up and not go?"

"Ava, we agreed."

"I know what we said. But I don't want to face him. Do you?"

Liam said nothing.

I spun away from him. "I can already imagine how it'll go. There's no way he'll be cool with it."

"We don't control his reaction. Just our own actions. That's important to remember."

"Well, his possible reaction scares me." I paced the short length of my living room.

"Ava—"

"Liam, you know him. He won't take it in stride. He'll be upset. With me, with you…" I stopped and faced him. "W-what if he—"

The words stuck in my throat, unable to verbalize them. The last thing I wanted was a falling out between Liam and my dad. They were the best of friends.

And that friendship was ruined because—

"Ava." Liam's smooth, commanding baritone rushed over my senses and chased away that thought. "Look at me."

I raised my gaze from my folded hands.

He'd come a step closer, and now every inhale carried his manly scent. If confidence was a cologne, it'd smell like that.

"It's going to be alright."

I tried to make myself believe that and it hadn't worked. It still wasn't working now. "He'll be mad, Liam."

"And?" He closed in on me, firm hands gripping my shoulders. "We hide forever because he'll be mad?"

I swallowed. "Liam…"

"We can do this, okay?"

I closed my eyes and pulled in a breath, trying to believe it. In an effort to calm my nerves, I remembered how things were just a couple of days ago.

Liam and I hung out together. Just two soon-to-be parents. The knowledge of our baby just between us.

That was bliss.

This was a nightmare.

"What if it all goes wrong?" My eyes popped open. I laid my hands on his chest. "What if he—"

"Ava, we cannot stop what we must do because of the possibilities."

"But he may not accept us and the baby."

"I don't expect him to right away. But we will allow him whatever he needs to get him there. If he needs time, he'll get time. If he needs to hit me to feel better—" his lip quirked "—then that's alright, too."

"Liam!" I frowned. "No one's hitting you."

He chuckled. "I'm just saying."

"How are you this calm?"

His eyes sobered. "I'm not."

A smile pulled at my lips and an answering one came from Liam.

"So, can we go? Are you ready?"

I took a long, deep breath and sighed. It did nothing to center me. I shrugged anyway. "Ready as I'll ever be."

Liam planted a kiss on my forehead and pulled me with him to the door.

The drive over was quiet. Every mile that brought us closer to my dad's house tightened the knot in my chest.

By the time we stopped in his driveway, it was a miracle I could still breathe.

Liam shut off the engine and slanted a look at me. It was early evening and the soft shadows fell across his face.

He'd been the picture of composure back at my apartment, but now, not so much. His gray eyes carried worry lines around them, and they burned with intensity.

"We should go in." His voice was deceptively normal, but I caught the strain in it.

That didn't help my confidence.

"Great. We're doing this. We're going in right now."

"Mm-hmm."

But I couldn't move.

"Ava?"

"Okay!" I spun to the backseat. "Let me just get—where's the dessert?"

"What?"

"Liam, I always bring dessert for Sunday dinner. Where is it?"

Liam blinked. "I didn't see any dessert at your place."

"Oh God." I fell back in my seat and wrapped my arms around my stomach. "I forgot. I got dressed then I…I sat down on the couch and googled how to tell a person unpleasant news…"

"Our child is not unpleasant news."

"Then afterward you came and I—" I turned to him. "I didn't get dessert, Liam!"

"It's just dessert. I'm sure Thomas won't mind."

"No, it's not just dessert! It's tradition. The way things have always been." My heart raced so fast I had to pull in slow, deep breaths. "If I don't have it, he'll know something is up."

"Well, something is up."

"Oh geez. This is going to be a disaster. We have to

turn around. We need to go back and get something, anything."

"Ava, no. Look at me." When I didn't comply, he cupped my cheek. Then he turned my head so my gaze was on his. "Your dad won't get mad over forgetting dessert, I promise."

I gulped. "You're sure?"

"Very." The line between his brows was at war with the smile on his lips. "It's all good, okay?"

"You think so?"

"I know so." His thumb ran over my cheek softly. "We'll get through this tonight."

I closed my eyes and absorbed his words and his touch. His presence calmed me. For what it was worth, I was glad I wasn't doing this alone.

"Ready?"

I blinked open and nodded.

Dad met us at the door with a wide smile. "Peanut!" He swept me into a hug and squeezed. "How are you?"

"I'm okay, Dad."

He let go and faced his friend. "Liam, you made it."

A sensation crowded my gut. Would Dad suspect something was up since Liam and I had shown up together?

My eyes snapped to his face. His smile was in place and genuine, with no suspicion in his eyes.

"Come in, you two. Dinner's ready."

Dad disappeared into the house. Liam and I shared a look before following after him.

We stood in the foyer, eyes still on each other. Dad went on speaking, but neither of us listened. I, for sure, knew I didn't hear a word.

All I could hear was my heartbeat and the ticking clock. Dad would soon discover the truth. And I was going to be the one to tell him.

It had to be done.

I grabbed my scarf, but my hands fumbled around it, tangling it.

"Should I help?"

My eyes shot to Liam. "No."

Dad was in the kitchen, but his booming voice carried over to us. If he saw us touching…

"You're going make it worse."

Liam ignored my protests and made quick work of removing my scarf.

I pulled in a breath, then skirted around him to hang it up. Liam did a one-eighty so I remained in his line of vision. Like he didn't want me to leave his sight.

That'd surely tell Dad something. *Isn't that what you want?*

I wasn't sure anymore.

I hugged my arms around myself, trying to get my shivering under control.

"God, Ava." Liam pulled close. He planted his hands on my arms. "Get it together."

I'm scared.

His eyes softened. "It'll be okay."

He rocked forward like he wanted to hold me. I wanted it, too. I started to drift toward him.

"What are you two doing standing there?"

Liam's hands fell from my arms like I was burning him.

Dad hadn't noticed. Or if he did, he didn't care. That's how much he trusted us.

"Come on, come on!" He waved us in. "The food's not going to eat itself."

I pushed myself forward despite the tightness in my chest.

Dad set out the dishes on the dinner table. This was the

part I always helped him with. Maybe sticking to our routine would ground me.

I picked up a place setting and started to lay it on the table.

"So, what have you been up to?"

My heart flew into my mouth and the plate slipped from my hand and slammed against the table.

"Ava?" Dad's brows knitted.

"Uh, nothing. Much."

His frown didn't ease. "I think you should sit."

"I think so, too." I took a seat.

I was still trying to pull in a calming breath when I felt a presence next to me. I turned and found Liam lowering himself into the chair beside me.

"What are you doing?" I whispered.

"Sitting."

"Don't—"

Dad returned with a pan of focaccia bread. "You won't guess what happened."

Liam and I didn't say a word.

"I got the delivery of the swiss cheese I'd been expecting for months. And it cleared out within three days. Can you believe it?"

I murmured a response but I doubted Dad heard me.

He put a slice of the bread on my plate and his. "Folks in Hannibal love it. But I've switched vendors so it wouldn't take too long to get here."

His eyes went to the empty spot opposite me and his brow rose. He'd expected Liam to sit there.

But he didn't say a word. Just rounded the table, placed Liam's plate, and dished his serving. Then topped them all with oil and vinegar.

"It's a brilliant product, I tell you." He rubbed his hands together as he took his seat. "Let's eat."

The meal looked delicious. Dad made the best focaccia bread I had ever tasted. But I couldn't bring myself to take a bite.

My stomach was a jumble of nerves. Nothing would stay in there, anyway. And I needed myself present for what we were about to do.

If I could disappear right now, I would. Or fast-forward to the end of the pregnancy. Maybe by then, my dad would be on board with it, and we could escape this difficult part—telling him.

But that wasn't possible.

He deserved the truth. And not from anyone. Not even from Liam.

It had to come from me. I owed him that much.

"What is up with you two?"

My gaze shot to Dad.

"You don't like the meal, is that it?" He looked between Liam and I. "You've been quiet all evening and you haven't touched your bread yet. Did I do something wrong?"

My heart squeezed. I looked at Liam.

His gaze held the same determination I felt.

It was time for me to tell Dad.

Chapter 24

Liam

Ava swallowed. She took a deep breath, then blew it out. She was gearing up to tell Thomas about us.

All evening, she believed she was more nervous than me. She had no idea. Right now, my heart was thundering in my chest.

But focusing on Ava allowed me remain present. Instead of drowning in my worries, wondering what the outcome of this night would be, I needed to support her.

She licked her lips. "Um…"

My heart clutched in sympathy for her. I reached under the table and placed a hand on her thigh. I felt her stiffen.

Thomas wouldn't see a thing. All his attention was focused on her face.

Knowing that, I rubbed her thigh softly. Her hand found mine and I laced our fingers and squeezed once.

You've got this.

She glanced at me. It was only a split second. But it

lasted long enough to see the gratitude in her eyes and the slight smile on her lips.

I smiled back, despite my wild heartbeat.

She was going to tell him. It wouldn't be just our secret anymore.

Thomas would know about the baby. About us. And he'd have every right to hate me.

Focus on Ava.

"Dad," she said in a small voice.

"Yes, Peanut." Thomas smiled.

Her hand shook and I held tighter.

"There's something I need to tell you."

"That my focaccia is terrible?" He pressed a hand to his chest. "Say it quickly. Come on, get it over with."

"Dad." Ava's voice cracked. "It's important."

Thomas heard it, too. He frowned and sat straighter. "This isn't about the bread, is it?"

Ava shook her head.

Thomas blinked and gave me a passing glance before returning to Ava. "What is it, then?"

She swallowed once more. "It's… It's about…" She sighed. "Well, promise me you won't get mad."

Thomas cracked a smile and leaned forward. "Ava, you can tell me anything. You know that."

My chest tightened. His eyes were adoring as he looked at his daughter. The woman I got pregnant.

Fuck. I really messed up.

I managed to breathe evenly as Ava nodded.

"Okay, here it goes." Her mouth opened, then shut.

That frown was creeping back onto Thomas's face.

"But first, Dad, what I'm about to tell you is big, okay?"

Thomas's forehead lined as his frown deepened.

"And it may not be what you expect, or what you want

to hear right now. But I need you to understand that I'm very happy."

My heart turned over. I looked at Ava. She was?

She'd been through a lot in the past few weeks. Had dealt with the pregnancy all on her own until I found out and acted like an ass. And even now, pushing through the anxiety to tell Thomas.

Was it possible she really was happy?

But the smile shining on her face was genuine. She looked down briefly, before looking back up at Thomas.

"I only hope that once you hear everything and have time to process it, you'll be happy for me, too."

I wish I could pull her into a hug and kiss her. But I settled for a hand squeeze. She was so brave and beautiful.

And a warmth weaved through my chest. The baby wasn't planned, but if I were given a choice now, Ava would be the one with whom I'd share the experience.

I was happy, too. Despite everything, it felt right. And hearing her say as much to her father thrilled me.

"Okay." Thomas's brows knotted. "What's all this about?"

My heart thudded as Ava's lips moved. I held my breath, braced for the inevitable.

"Dad, I'm pregnant."

Thomas's brows shot up, his eyes not leaving Ava. We stayed that way for several seconds, but it felt like an eternity.

"Dad?" Ava whispered.

"You're pregnant?" Thomas finally spoke.

"Yes." Ava's hand clutched mine so tightly I lost the feeling in my fingers.

Suddenly, the frown on Thomas's face fell away and a big grin shone through. "You're pregnant!?"

"Um, yes."

"You're pregnant!" Thomas shot to his feet.

Ava jumped and leaned back into me. "Dad…"

"Oh my gosh, this is big news!" He paced behind his chair. "I can't—I'm going to be a grandpa."

"Dad."

"You're having a baby. Ava! How long have you known? My little Peanut is going to be a mom!" He wiped his hands down his face, shaking his head. "Just yesterday you were running around in diapers. Now you're a mom."

Ava's chuckle was hesitant. "That's not everything."

Her words didn't get past his excitement.

"We should do something." He paced, then stopped and stared over our heads. "We must celebrate! Yes, a party."

"Dad—"

"Ava, don't you get it?" He stared at her with bright eyes. "You're having a baby. We're getting a little addition to our family. It's the greatest thing ever! I've had my fingers crossed for the longest time."

"Dad, you need to… What? Longest time?"

"Uh-huh." He nodded quickly. "Now that dream is coming to life. You're having—"

"A baby, yes, Dad. But that's not all."

"It's not?" His smile broadened. "Are there two?"

"Dad!" Ava chided. "Sit."

Thomas dropped into his chair, still grinning. "What is it, Peanut?"

He was expecting more good news. I wished we could stop at that point, and leave him deliriously happy. But now was probably the best time.

Since he was so happy about the baby, the revelation of who the father was shouldn't be so bad.

I could only hope.

"There's more."

"You've said so." Thomas beamed. "Spill it, Ava. I can't wait."

She gulped. "Um, okay, so… You know I can't make a baby on my own."

He chuckled. "Of course not, that'd be a medical miracle. Right, Liam?"

I couldn't get a word past my constricted throat, so I nodded.

"Yes…" Ava said slowly. "So, about my baby's father…"

"Is it the mystery boyfriend?" Thomas leaned in.

I frowned. Mystery boyfriend?

"Y-yes," Ava replied.

Mystery… Oh, me. I was the mystery.

"Oh, great! I've been looking forward to meeting him. I just didn't want to push it until you were ready. Now can I meet him?"

Ava looked down. A beat passed before her gaze came up and traveled between Thomas and me.

"You've met him."

Thomas shook his head. "I don't think I have. You haven't brought him home. I—"

"It's Liam."

My stomach grew tight. I held my breath, waiting for the outburst. Only, it didn't happen as I expected.

Thomas didn't fly into a rage and punch my teeth out. Instead, he burst into laughter, slapping a fist on the table.

"Oh, Ava." He threw his head back. "You got me. For a moment there, I believed you. But no, that's impossible. You got me good. Try again." He managed to stop laughing and faced Ava. "Who's the father?"

Ava blinked and glanced at me, then back at her dad. "It's Liam, Dad. I'm not kidding."

Thomas's smile fell as he looked between us both. Whatever he saw was quickly stealing his joy.

I swallowed.

Ava turned to me, her voice quiet. "Liam is the father of my baby. I'm pregnant with his child. We didn't plan it. It just happened."

Her hand squeezed mine and a note of contentment worked through me. But it wasn't enough to forget reality.

Thomas had gone very still. And even as my eyes were on Ava, I was very aware of him. Of his silence.

He heard every word. Now he believed it. And was processing it.

"We know it's a lot for you to take in." She turned back to Thomas. "And we understand if you're mad, but—"

"Mad?" Thomas rose in a slow, steady movement, his body almost shaking. "Mad?"

His eyes flashed behind his glasses. Gone was the ordinary man that ran a grocery store and doted on his daughter. Thomas the college football linebacker had returned.

He clenched his fists, staring us down. "I'm not mad, Ava. I'm livid!"

Ava stood, raising her hands. "Dad, calm down."

"Don't tell me to calm down!"

She jumped. I rose and placed steadying hands on her shoulders.

Bad move.

Thomas's eyes narrowed on the me, his eyes darkening. "You! How dare you touch her."

Ava anticipated his rushing toward me and moved forward. "Dad, no!"

"How dare you put your hands on her? Huh? How dare you?!" Thomas kicked Ava's chair.

I caught it just before it could hit me.

"You bastard."

"Dad, please!" Ava cried, grabbing his cardigan with both hands. "He didn't know who I was when we met. We didn't plan it, I promise."

"Ava, stay out of this."

"No, you're not listening."

"You are not listening! He is twice your age. He knows you're my daughter and he chose to take advantage of you."

"No, Dad. That's not what happened. I—"

"You're not good enough for her!"

"Dad—"

"He isn't good for you, Peanut. Can't you see?"

A strangled sound left Ava. "Please—"

"That's why you came back, isn't it? You came back to use my daughter. She's a young naive small-town girl and you think because she's my daughter I'd let you have her, huh? That's why you knocked her up, right?"

Thomas tried to get past Ava but she stood firmly, thwarting his efforts.

I stood in the same spot. Whatever he wanted to do, he was within his rights. I couldn't even find the words to defend myself.

Anger and frustration made his face go red. "Liam, I fucking trusted you! She's my child."

"Dad, please, it's not like you think." Ava pulled at his cardigan. "It was my choice."

"This was your choice?!" Thomas jabbed a finger in my direction. "Then you're not thinking."

"Stop! How can you speak like this? I am not a child. I chose to sleep with Liam. I chose to keep the baby."

Thomas's eyes narrowed on her. "Your choice?"

I stepped forward. It was better when his anger was directed at me, not her.

"Well, then, I'm the fool." His gaze snapped to mine.

"You two adults are making choices and I'm being the unreasonable asshole."

"I didn't say—"

"Get out."

"What?"

"Get the hell out of my house!"

Ava fell back. I grabbed her arms to keep her upright.

"Get out, both of you!" Thomas yelled.

Ava tried to speak, maybe ask him to reconsider. But his face was beet red. He was past being reasonable right now.

"Come on, let's go." I pulled her toward the door.

She stared at her dad, her eyes frozen in horror. "Please, Dad."

Thomas didn't budge. He watched as I grabbed her purse and scarf, hustling us to the door.

"Dad! You can't do this."

We were at the door when Thomas spoke.

"This is the last time I want to see you two together. If I ever see you again, Liam, you'll be sorry."

We stepped onto the porch and the door slammed in our faces.

Chapter 25

Ava

I stared out the passenger window, my entire body numb. We were across town, far away from my dad. But my head was still stuck in the dining room under the storm clouds of his anger.

I heaved a sigh and sank into the seat. If I could turn back time, I'd...

Not tell him?

Do what?

Nothing! There was nothing I could have done differently to make my dad less infuriated.

I shut my eyes against the image of his angry red face. But doing that only made it stand out clearer.

At first, he funneled his rage at Liam. He certainly would have thrown a punch at him if I hadn't been there.

But then, he turned on me.

I swallowed thickly, squeezing a fistful of my dress.

He looked at me like he'd never seen me before. Like I was a stranger he didn't recognize.

He hated me now.

Just thinking it produced a whimper I couldn't hide. I'd used all my optimism and energy on my dad, telling him about the baby and enduring the fallout afterward. Anything that happened now, I didn't have the energy to fight it.

"Ava." Liam's voice whisked away the jumble of thoughts in my head. "Are you alright?"

"He hates me," I whispered.

"He doesn't."

"Yes, he does."

"No."

"I wish I could have… If I'd only…" My throat tightened. "That went horribly wrong. Maybe if I would've—"

"There's nothing we could have done differently, Ava. Thomas got mad because that was his earnest reaction. We can't control how people react."

"He kicked us out of his house!"

"In the heat of the moment. But I'm certain once he's had time to think about it, he'll come around."

I shook my head even before he finished speaking. "I don't think so. I've never seen him that angry. Have you?"

"Ava…"

"No, really." I shifted in my seat so I faced him. "Have you?"

Tight lines traced the corners of his eyes and his lips pressed into a flat line.

Seconds passed and he had no response for me.

"I thought as much." I dropped back in the seat and stared out at the brake lights moving in front of us. "He'll never speak to us again."

"It'll be alright, Ava."

"Just because you say it over and over doesn't mean it'll

happen!" I pressed my hands to my face, instant regret rushing through me.

Liam wasn't at fault. I shouldn't have raised my voice. I was just so frustrated that I—

"Come back home with me."

I raised my gaze to meet his. "What?"

"I don't want you to be alone tonight."

That was sweet. Especially after I just shouted at him. But...

I shook my head. "I'd like to go to Linea's, please."

The car's engine was the only sound for a few moments.

"Alright," Liam said evenly.

Guilt twisted in my gut. We'd just endured a difficult evening. It made sense to process it together.

But being with him after all that happened seemed wrong. Like my Dad's anger was justified.

He never wanted to see us together again.

Not that he had followed us and would know where I spent the night. I just needed some time apart.

"Are you mad?" I murmured.

"No, I'm not. Ava, I can't be mad at you."

His words spread a balm over the guilt tearing through me. At least one person I cared about didn't see me as a villain.

"It's just what I need right now, some time apart. I just need a bit of space."

Liam side-eyed me. "I understand, Ava. It's alright."

He didn't sound like it was alright. I felt the need to further explain myself, but I resisted. There was nothing more to say.

I gave him Linea's address. Every mile that brought us closer to her place seemed to push us farther apart.

The truck came to a stop in front of her building. It felt

wrong to leave him like this, especially because there seemed to be many unsaid words hanging between us.

"Liam, are you okay?"

He nodded, gray eyes fixed on me. "I'm fine."

I swallowed, dread filling me. This felt like an end. And I didn't want any endings where Liam was concerned.

"H-how are you always so calm?"

A sad smile stretched his lips. "I'm not."

I smiled back and waited.

Maybe he'd touch me. Give me a peck on the forehead. A gentle squeeze of my hand.

Anything.

Seconds passed.

Nothing happened.

He just stared at me intently, as if to make sure I was okay.

I forced a smile and opened the door. "Good night, Liam."

I didn't wait for his response. My feet hit the sidewalk and I moved to Linea's door. Then I paused and turned.

Liam's truck was still there. He looked at me, brows furrowed.

For some reason, my chin started to tremble and my heart hammered. I ducked my head and knocked. Linea opened the door so fast, it was as though she had been waiting for me.

"Oh, Ava."

I let her pull me into her arms.

"I messed up." My voice was muffled against her shoulder.

"Hey, it's okay." She ran her hands down my hair and back.

I pulled in a deep breath, willing myself to believe it.

Seconds passed before the familiar rumble of Liam's

truck kicked up. I stood straighter and looked toward the door. The sound carried for a bit, then faded.

I squeezed my eyelids shut and forced the tears back. I was my choice to stay at Linea's.

"Come on." Linea looped her arm through mine and pulled me into her home.

I followed, only finding the strength to shuffle one foot in front of the other.

Linea eased me into a chair by the kitchen table. "Hungry?"

"Yeah, we didn't even get to eat dinner."

"Yikes," Linea muttered. She moved around the kitchen, then stopped. "So, it looks like I don't have any real food. Just ice cream."

"That's fine."

"Cool."

A tub of ice cream appeared in front of me with a spoon sticking out of it. I dug in and filled my mouth with the cold chocolate caramel treat.

I could have been eating dirt for all I knew. Instead of enjoying the yummy deliciousness, all I could do was replay through my head the terrible evening I'd experienced.

A few moments of silence passed before Linea spoke. "Want to tell me how it went?"

Maybe speaking about it out loud would bring me some peace. "We arrived at my dad's early this evening…"

Linea took the seat next to me, watching me with careful eyes. A couple of days ago, I called and told her what Liam and I decided. She had always been in support of telling Dad.

What none of us anticipated, though, was how badly he would take it.

When I narrated how he reacted, Linea gasped.

"So, that's how it went. Dad hates me now and I can't even look at Liam because…well, how can we ever face my dad again? I didn't want this to happen. I didn't—"

The tears I sniffed back all evening poured out of me now. I pressed my hands to my face, sobbing.

Linea had no words for me. She leaned forward and wrapped her arms around my shoulders.

I cried until my tears were dried up and I was left with only a shuddering breath. "I don't know what to do, Lin. Where do I go from here?"

"Hey…" Linea brushed back my hair and tipped my face up. "Oh my."

I wiped my eyes. "I look bad, huh?"

"Hideous."

Laughter cracked out of me, then my vision blurred as the tears started again.

"Oh, dear." Linea rubbed my shoulder. "It'll be alright."

"It won't. You didn't see how mad my dad was. He'll never get past the fact that Liam's the father. And if he can't accept Liam, will he accept our baby?"

"Of course, he will. Don't think like that, Ava." She scooted forward. "Your dad loves you. And based on what you told me, he was mostly worried that Liam was taking advantage of you."

"But he's not!"

"It might take some time for your dad to realize that."

I sniffed and wiped my cheeks. "You should have seen his face. He looked wounded, like I had betrayed him."

She squeezed my shoulder.

"He was ready to punch Liam. They're best friends! If I would have just stayed away from Liam that first night, all of this wouldn't have happened."

"Do you really mean that?"

My lip quirked. "No, not really. I'd probably do it again. Maybe ask him to—"

"Um, no." Linea hopped off her chair. "That's where I draw the line."

I chuckled. "Wait, don't you want to hear—"

"Nope. I'm not listening to your sexcapades between you and your—"

"Baby's father."

"Baby's father," she repeated.

Reality snuck back in and wrapped me up in its clutches. I couldn't go back and change the past. And I didn't want to.

Liam was like no other man I'd dated, and having a baby with him was a dream come true.

I only wished I'd handled things with my dad in a better way.

"I didn't mean to keep it from him." I turned to Linea, who now stood by the sink. "I was just scared of how he'd react. And now... It's worse than I ever expected."

"You can't control how your dad acts, Ava."

I sighed. "I guess. I just wish he didn't feel like I've betrayed him. All my life, he's always been there for me. I told him everything until this."

Linea sat down next to me and took my hand in hers. "Your dad treasures you. You're the most important thing in his world. And I don't think this will get in the way of your relationship permanently."

I eyed her.

"He already loves your baby. What parent talks of throwing a party to celebrate the news?"

A feeling of relief passed through me, but it didn't last. The memory of dad's fury was too strong.

"Look, he's entitled to his reaction. But when all is said

and done, I think you'll find that he'll be there to support you."

I raised a disbelieving brow. "Really?"

Linea's smile was brilliant. "I know it. Just you watch."

I sagged back in the chair, trying to picture Dad accepting Liam and me as a couple, and our baby. Because we were the entire package; he couldn't accept us and exclude Liam.

You touched her. He took advantage of you. Get out of my house!

I shut my eyes, trying to block out the words.

He would never let it go.

"Ava?"

I blinked and my friend's face came into focus. "But what if he doesn't? What if he never comes around?"

Linea didn't have a response.

Chapter 26

Liam

It'd been three days since that fateful dinner. Three days since we had received the full blast of Thomas's anger. Three days since I dropped Ava off at Linea's house.

Three days since my heart broke.

It's a funny thing, getting your heart broken. It's ironic because I thought I didn't have a heart.

But I learned.

The pain in my chest wasn't from carrying furniture around my house, rearranging rooms that didn't need it. The ache in my head wasn't from working overtime, obsessing over things. The sleepless nights weren't from too much coffee.

It ached everywhere, getting your heart broken.

That's what I learned.

It also became all-consuming. Made a man distracted and useless at work.

And I tried to push past it. I tried to be there for my patients.

But when one of them pointed out that maybe I was the one who needed fixing, I threw in the towel. I locked myself in my office and considered my options.

One, do nothing but wallow and suffer.

Two, go behind Thomas's back and see Ava anyway. But then endure the guilt afterward.

Three, speak to Thomas. Lay everything out in the open and take whatever comes.

The last one was the most intimidating. But that's what I needed to do.

It'd only been three days and it felt like a lifetime.

Ava had quickly become the center of my universe. I saw her everywhere. In everything. Just a few days without her smile and I was miserable.

Cooper, you've got it bad.

I needed to fix this, ASAP.

Ava didn't want to see me now that Thomas had forbidden it. Probably to respect her dad's wishes. Or prevent me from getting a broken nose if Thomas saw us together.

But I couldn't live like this.

I'd give anything to see her, hold her. I missed the way she'd rest her head on my chest, and I'd inhale her sweet feminine scent and feel her lush curves against me.

I had to get my girl back.

I had ruined her relationship with her dad. And if we saw each other behind Thomas's back it would only make things worse when he found out. I needed to set things right with him before pursuing anything with her.

It felt like the end, the way we'd left things on Sunday. But it couldn't be over for us. Not only did I need her like I needed my next breath, but I also wanted to be in my child's life, too. Fuck, I wanted to be in both their lives.

And Ava would never settle for only having only me *or* Thomas in her life. She'd want peace between us.

On my way out, I gave the nurse instructions to close up. Just in case I took a fist to the face and couldn't see my patients.

I clutched the wheel with shaky hands, tearing down the road toward Thomas's home. I glanced in the side mirror and caught my reflection. A confidence I didn't feel stared back at me.

How are you always so calm?

Soft and sweet, her voice lingered in my head. I missed her. So much.

I buried whatever hesitation I had and pushed down on the gas pedal.

It's now or never.

The late evening sun shone on Thomas's home. I came to a stop in the driveway behind his car.

Before I could reconsider my decision, I stepped out of the car. I made my way up to the front door, drew in a deep breath, then knocked.

The door creaked open slowly and the lump in my throat grew. I fisted my hands and stood my ground.

Thomas stood in the doorway. The scowl that covered his face couldn't be mistaken. He wasn't happy to see me.

"What are you doing here?" He took a step forward and filled the doorway with his bulk.

He'd foregone his usual cardigan for a T-shirt that spread across his chest and clung to his biceps.

I wasn't intimidated. Not one bit.

"Didn't I tell you to get the hell out of my house? Why did you think you could come back here?"

"We need to talk."

"You have nothing—" he stabbed a finger at my chest

"—nothing at all I want to hear. And we sure as hell have nothing to talk about!"

"If you won't hear me out for the sake of our friend-ship, think of Ava!"

His face became murderous. "Don't say her name."

"This is killing her." *It's killing me.* "You probably hate me right now. Hell, I'd hate me, too, if I was in your shoes. I fucked up. I know. But we need to fix this for her sake."

Thomas shut his eyes, the tendon in his neck jumping.

I waited.

"For Ava."

I nodded, even though he couldn't see me.

He opened his eyes and threw me a scathing look. "You better have a damn good reason for why this happened."

He turned and headed back inside, leaving the door ajar.

I glanced behind me before following him into the house. Here's to hoping I could convince him my reason was a good one.

Thomas stalked to the kitchen. He grabbed the refrig-erator door and jerked it open.

He rummaged around and grabbed a bottle of beer. His fingers grazed a second but he withdrew his hand and slammed the door close. He popped off the cap.

After a long swallow, he slammed the bottle down and folded his beefy arms across his chest. "Start talking."

Here goes nothing…

"I never planned this, Thomas."

"You mean me finding out you were sleeping with my daughter?"

I cringed. "I didn't know who she was. I was new in Hannibal, and I went to Busters. That's where we met."

He frowned. "That was before you came over for dinner."

"Yes."

I clenched my teeth over my ignorance. I should have seen the resemblance. But Ava swept me away that first night.

And every day since.

I brought my head back to the present. "I should have known, but it'd been years since I was here. I had no idea who she was, Thomas."

He looked down at the island, his brows knotted. "I guess you couldn't have known—" His gaze shot up. "But you knew who she was the night you came over for dinner?"

I gritted my teeth. "I did."

"And you kept seeing her after that?!"

"No—not at first. It was supposed to be a one-time thing."

"You wanted to use her and leave her?"

"Jesus, Thomas! She's a woman, not a child, and if she wants to be casual, that's her decision!"

If Thomas's eyes could shoot daggers, I'd be dead. But he didn't respond.

A few beats passed before I continued. "We stopped seeing each other. It worked for a while, until it didn't."

"And this whole time, you didn't see fit to tell me? You didn't think I'd want to know my daughter was pregnant?" His brows lifted. "Oh my God, I'm such an idiot."

He paced the kitchen, muttering, "The dizziness, the near-fainting... When did you find out?"

It was no use trying to sugarcoat it. The longer this conversation went on, the more I realized how betrayed he likely felt.

"The night you brought her over."

"Oh God." He pressed both hands to his face. "My poor Peanut."

Guilt wound through my chest. He'd been worried that night, but I'd given him empty lies to distract him.

"You!" He suddenly looked up, rage burning in his gaze. "Tell me why the fuck I should let this go! You lied to me. Why should I believe you now?"

"I was respecting her wishes. I was looking out for her, Thomas!"

"By screwing her? You said you didn't plan any of it. Do you even want the baby? Do you even care about her?"

The accusation sent a knife through my heart. "Of course, I fucking do!"

I was raising my voice. I never did that.

If Ava could see me now, she'd never call me calm again. I should back down, and work things out peacefully. But his assumptions angered me.

"It might have started casually. But we're not just hooking up. Hell, it's never been that."

Even that first night, I didn't want to leave her. I'd looked at her beautiful face, her lashes fanning her cheeks, and thought I was a fool to walk away.

"I care about Ava…" I swallowed. "Deeply."

"Don't sell me bullshit, Cooper."

"I fucking wish it was bullshit. Then maybe I could finally do something other than think of her all day."

His eyebrows pulled together.

I doubled back quickly. "What I'm trying to say, Thomas, is that even if given a choice, I wouldn't change the last few weeks. The only thing I would do differently is not keep it from you. But Ava? I cannot wish her away. She's an incredible woman with a huge heart. She has the best laugh I've ever heard. And she's brilliant."

A smile stole over my face. "We talk for hours and she makes me laugh. I've never had that. I've never had someone who accepts everything I am and sets me at ease

Doctor Everything

in every way. Someone with whom I can be completely comfortable."

I swallowed past the thickness in my throat. "So... I know how this looks. I know how it may seem. But I treasure her. I'm dedicated to taking care of her. Making her feel safe and loved. And giving her and our baby everything they need to be happy and whole."

Thomas's gaze stayed on mine, his eyes doubtful.

"And I understand the way everything unfolded has hurt you, Thomas. Believe me, I do. And I'm sorry. I never meant for it to turn out this way. You're my best friend and I don't want to ruin our friendship. But I love Ava so damn much. I can't walk away."

Thomas's brow lifted and he croaked, "Love?"

I swallowed. I had no idea I'd said the words. He'd surely clobber me now.

But there was no way I could deny it.

I nodded. "Yes. I'm completely at her mercy."

Chapter 27

Ava

My phone buzzed on the coffee table. Farther than an arm's length away.

I stretched for it and my muscles screamed in protest. Lying around on the couch from dawn till dusk didn't make for very flexible joints.

Snack wrappers tumbled to the floor and my blanket fell away.

It'd probably be Linea checking to make sure I wasn't having another meltdown.

That was my MO this past week. Mourning the ruined relationship with my dad while avoiding Liam. I had barely gotten by.

When the weekend arrived, it hit me that today—Sunday—would be the one-week anniversary of everything falling apart.

Linea was there when I broke down, tears filling my eyes. She'd held me and asked if there was anything she could do.

Everything I wanted—everything I needed, she couldn't give.

So I claimed I'd be alright.

But I was far from it.

I woke up this morning with a gaping hole where my heart used to be. I sat in front of the TV, ate snacks, and napped.

Yet, I couldn't avoid the memories. Dad's anger. Leaving Liam. Avoiding him all week.

Now, to reassure Linea.

I finally reached the phone and slid my thumb across the screen, already forming the words that would set her at ease.

But it wasn't Linea who sent the text.

It was Liam.

My heart skipped a beat. What did he want? My fingers fumbled as I clicked the message open.

Come over to my house.

That was it.

I frowned.

Did he forget my dad didn't want us together? Was he drunk texting?

I'd never seen Liam drunk. He was always poised. Always in control of himself.

Always intentional.

If he asked to see me, he meant it.

Could I risk it, though?

Dad would hurt Liam if he saw us together. That was the last thing I wanted.

I didn't want to resent my dad and I also didn't want Liam injured.

Despite this, I was tempted.

I missed Liam. I missed his deep, rumbling laugh. I

missed his gray eyes that went from soft to stormy in a flash. I missed his touch.

A need greater than reason rose inside me.

Even if it made Dad mad, I couldn't stay away. I had to see him.

I jumped into action, racing to the bathroom and tossing off my clothes. After a quick shower, I threw on a simple dress and sandals. Then tied my hair up into a messy bun.

I drew my purse strap over my shoulder and stopped in front of the door. I read the text one last time.

It wouldn't be impossible that I imagined it because I missed him so much. But there it was, word for word.

I took a deep breath and stepped out into the warm evening.

A short drive later, I climbed the porch steps to Liam's front door, exhaled, then knocked. Everything was quiet but I found myself scanning the area, paranoid that my dad would see me here.

But no one was around.

I still wasn't eager to keep standing out here.

Where are you, Liam?

I knocked again.

The door finally opened.

I wasn't sure what I expected, but it wasn't seeing Liam looking so happy. Lines framed his gray eyes and his lips pulled up in a cheeky grin.

My stomach flipped, but I tamped down that feeling immediately. How could he be so cheerful when I was such a mess?

"What's going on, Liam. Why did you invite me here?"

"To see me." His lips twitched. "Is that so bad?"

My stupid stomach dropped. I wanted to kiss that smile off his face until he was moaning my name.

"It would be if my dad found out."

He chuckled like it was nothing and took my hand.

My body melted at his touch but I held my head high. Wasn't he worried about, well, everything?

"Liam, I don't think I should be here."

The door shut behind me.

"You'll see." His fingers curled around mine and he led me toward the stairs.

"Liam."

"Hey." He stopped at the foot of the stairs and faced me. "Do you trust me?"

I looked up into gray eyes. My heart thumped with a resounding yes. "This is reckless."

He smiled. "Come on."

His carefree attitude had my belly alight with butterflies, but I couldn't forget all the things that could go wrong.

Namely, my dad finding out I was here.

"Where are we going?" I asked as we reached the top step.

His answer was a gentle tug that led us down the hallway.

Was he taking us to his bedroom?

But instead of his bedroom, he stopped by a spare room and pushed the door open.

"Liam, what is—" My eyes caught the figure in the room and my heart lurched. "Dad!"

He stared at me.

I whisked my hand out of Liam's and pressed myself to the door jamb to hold myself up.

"Dad, hi. What are you—" I looked at Liam, then back to my dad. "It's not what you think. I just—" My brows pulled together. "Wait, what are you doing here? I thought you were angry at us, at Liam. What's happening?"

A slow smile tugged at my father's face, his brown eyes shining behind his glasses. He stepped forward. "I asked Liam to invite you over."

"Is this a test?"

"No." He pushed his glasses up his nose.

He only did that when he was nervous.

"Dad, what is it?"

"Well." He cleared his throat. "We put this together and we wanted to show you."

Put what together? I followed his gesture and took in the room.

"Oh!" I took a step inside and my mouth hung open. "What—what did you do?"

"It's a nursery for the baby," Liam answered from behind me. "What do you think?"

Tears filled my eyes. I spun in a circle, seeing everything in one sweep.

"It's gorgeous! But how?"

Liam placed firm hands on my shoulders, grounding me. "Your dad helped bring it all together."

"Dad." My voice broke.

I ran across the room and jumped into his arms. He held me against him.

"I'm sorry, Ava. I'm so sorry."

Tears leaked out of the corners of my eyes. "I should have told you about me and Liam. But I was so scared."

"And I proved you right. I should never have acted that way." He pulled back and cupped my cheeks, wiping my face with his thumbs. "You know I only want what's best for you, don't you?"

I nodded, fighting back a fresh batch of tears.

"I was just afraid Liam was using you."

"And now?"

Dad looked past me. "I'm willing to believe otherwise."

"Oh, Dad." I wrapped my arms around his neck. "Thank you."

"No, thank you for not being mad at me."

"Oh no." I pulled back. "I'm still mad at you."

"What?"

"Mm-hmm. You owe me a fresh batch of focaccia and all the other goodies I missed out on."

Dad grinned. "Anything you want. For you and the little one." His eyes dropped to my belly.

I smiled, then my gaze slipped behind him and my mouth turned into a giant "O." "What is that?" I went to the wall.

"We had Meghan paint a mural when she was in town this weekend," Dad explained.

The Meghan? Oh my goodness, it's gorgeous."

My eyes slipped away from the cream, pink, and blue mural and fell on the wooden crib. It was carved with stylish designs and laid with a soft mattress.

"This is so precious." I could picture my baby snuggled in it.

"Liam had it specially designed." Dad pressed a button and a border kicked out. "To ensure the baby's safety."

"Oh, wow." I pressed a hand to my chest. "Any more and my heart is going to explode."

Dad instantly frowned. "Should we be worried?"

I laughed. "No."

"Well, then, there's more. Liam ordered a rocking chair." Dad hurried to stand by a corner next to the window. "It'll sit right here."

Soft evening sunlight spilled through the window. It already looked so peaceful.

I turned to Liam, my heart full and spilling over. "Thank you."

A smile tugged at his lips. "Anything for you."

"Really?"

"Always." He nodded, kissing my forehead and drawing me into his arms.

We gazed at each other for a full minute, then Dad reminded us of his presence by clearing his throat.

I pulled back, not yet used to the fact that we no longer had to hide.

Dad bent to pick up a bag. "I won't be in your way much longer."

"Dad..." I laughed.

"Nah, I understand." Dad drew close and pulled me into a hug.

He lingered longer than usual before pulling back. A look passed between him and Liam, and Liam inclined his head.

My brows furrowed, but I put it out of my mind. At least they weren't fighting.

Dad was almost out the door when he turned. "Dinner is on, as always, tonight. See you both in a couple of hours."

My eyes teared up. After last Sunday, I treasured every moment of harmony together.

"See you soon," I called out.

Once my dad left, I faced Liam. "How?"

He chuckled and circled his arms around my waist. My body met his and a thrill ran through me.

"It took a bit of explaining to clear the air."

"No punches?"

He laughed and shook his head. "None. We're good."

"Liam." I sighed. "I'm so relieved. I was scared."

"Never again, princess." He ran his hands down my arms.

I shut my eyes and placed my face in the crook of his neck. "We'll be fine?"

"Yes." His voice washed over me. "You, me, and our baby."

I smiled and kissed his neck. His fingers dug into my hips, so I kissed him again.

"I've missed you," I whispered.

"I've missed you more."

I was airborne the next second.

I yelped and grabbed onto his shirt. His laughter was warm as he carried me into his bedroom.

My back hit the bed but I sat up immediately, reaching for his belt buckle. He helped me work it off and then stepped out of his pants.

His hands were on me a second later. He pulled my zipper down and my dress fell off, leaving me in just my bra and panties.

Liam's eyes darkened. "Take it off. All of it," he rasped.

I did as he asked, getting naked in record time. When I looked back up, he was completely nude, too.

I couldn't help it. I reached for him and sighed as I caressed his bare skin.

He cupped my face and kissed my lips. We both groaned as our tongues tangled. Liam eased us onto the bed and covered me with his body.

It'd been a long week. I had thought we were over. That there was no going back.

And now, experiencing all of him after the fear and anxiety, I held nothing back.

I eased my legs open and Liam's hard length came to rest where I needed him the most.

"Ava," he whispered my name like a prayer, then sank himself deep.

A moan broke from my lips and I wrapped my legs around his waist.

He rocked inside me, brushed my hair back, and kissed the shell of my ear.

"I love you so much, Ava."

A shocked gasp left me. But that quickly turned into a moan as Liam changed angles and stroked deeper into me.

Before I knew it, my back arched and I was crying out. Seconds later, his liquid heat filled me up and we collapsed onto the bed.

Liam pulled me against him and kissed my temple.

I turned in his arms and rose on my elbow so I could see his face. "What did you say?"

He gave me a warm smile. "I love you."

I just stared into his eyes, not quite believing the words.

"I mean it, Ava. I love you."

My heart warmed. "Are you sure you're not just saying that because of the baby?"

He chuckled. "I love our baby, too. But I don't only love the life we created, princess. I love *you*. Your giving heart, your freckled face, your sweet nature, your everything. All of you."

I choked on a tear and buried my face in his chest. "Oh, Liam. I love you, too."

Epilogue

Liam

One year later

A light rain pattered on the roof and slid down the window. I blinked and turned over in bed.

My eyes fell on Ava's bare skin, half covered with the sheets. My cock jerked to life. It always did when I looked at her.

I pushed the feeling aside and swept a hand down her back.

She made an adorable sleepy sound, but remained at rest.

Good.

I rolled over, pulled out my bedside drawer, and picked up the small box inside. I popped it open. The square-cut jewel reflected the dim light coming in through the sheer curtains.

All week, I'd been waiting for the perfect moment. I even had a date night planned, but Wesley, our rosy-cheeked, dark-haired son, chose that evening to come down with a fever.

He was fine the next couple of hours, but by then it was late and the mood was gone. We ended up staying in and watching a movie. While it was nice, it wasn't the setting I wanted.

But I could wait no longer.

I turned to see her face relaxed in slumber. No better time than now, before the day really began.

She breathed heavily and turned over, reaching for me. Her face burrowed against my chest and a small smile played on her lips. Then she settled in again and resumed sleeping.

I swiped the stray hair that rested on her cheek and hated myself for it, but kissed her lips.

That always woke her up.

She needed more rest. But I needed to do this now. If not, we'd be plunged into a day of dirty diapers, burp clothes, and loads of laundry, with little free time.

Ava's response to my kiss was instant. The hand on my chest curled and her lips parted.

"Liam," she said in her breathy morning voice.

"I'm here, princess." I kissed each cheek and then her eyelids.

She laughed, her nose wrinkling and her eyes fluttering open. "Did you wake me up?"

"I did."

"Is Wesley alright?"

"Yes."

"Then why? These fifteen minutes before he gets up

are heaven. There better be a good reason." She snuggled back under the covers, closing her eyes again.

I swallowed, my throat suddenly full of emotion. "There is, I think."

"What is it?"

I popped open the box and placed it between us.

"Open your eyes, Ava."

She moaned a complaint but cracked her eyes open anyway. When she saw me, a smile spread across her lips.

My heart constricted. "Ava."

"Yes, Liam?"

"It's been a crazy year."

"I know. I've been here, too."

I laughed weakly. "Yes, and when I came to Hannibal, my plan was to escape my crazy schedule and settle into a quiet life."

"Wesley had other plans for you."

Laughter bubbled out of me. My gaze dropped to the ring she'd still not seen and back up to her face. "And that's okay. It's better than okay. It's the best thing I could have hoped for."

"Oh, Liam." She cupped my face.

I shut my eyes, pressing my cheek to her hand and absorbing her warm touch. "What I'm saying is, it seemed like I never really lived before you. Before this."

I opened my eyes to meet hers, now filled with tears. I whisked the moisture away with my thumbs.

"And I just wanted to say thank you."

She giggled. "You woke me up to say thank you? You're a sentimental man, Dr. Cooper."

I sucked in a breath. "And, I also want to say, or um, ask…if it's no trouble, I'd love it if you would keep making my life what it is now until…forever. And if I make you happy, too, I'd love to keep doing that."

EMMA BLAKE

Her smile faded and she frowned.

"Well, um, sorry. That's a very convoluted way to ask if you'll marry me."

"What?" Her brows lifted.

"Marry me, Ava." I lifted the box.

Her eyes fell on the ring and her chin trembled. She ignored the jewelry and dove straight for me. Her legs straddled me and she buried her face in my chest.

"Yes! Oh yes, Liam. I'll marry you."

Warmth exploded inside me. I hugged her close and kissed her forehead, unable to speak past the tightness in my throat.

Ava sat up and placed her left hand in my right. With my heart full, I slipped the ring on her finger.

She held it up, a big smile on her face, then she rested on my chest once more.

This time, her lips found mine.

I wrapped an arm around her lower back and the other behind her neck and kissed her until we were both breathless.

Her body grew restless and she ground her center against me.

The kiss shifted from slow and sweet to an urgency that had me tangling my hands in her hair.

She moaned and bared her neck to me. I kissed the soft flesh and sucked. Her body rocked harder, wetness spreading on my shaft.

"Put my cock inside you, baby girl. Let daddy fill that hungry pussy."

Her back bowed and she trembled. "Mmm, yes, daddy."

Her hand curled around my cock and her thumb swiped the head, spreading the precum over the tip.

A groan fell from my lips and I bit down on her

shoulder.

She shivered and sank down an inch. "Oh, daddy."

"Yes, princess."

"You feel so good."

I grabbed her waist, drugged by her needy voice. "Take me deeper. It'll feel better."

Ava had just begun to take more of me when a small cry rang out. We both paused, waiting. Nothing happened.

She resumed when a loud wailing filled the air.

"Ah, damn." She collapsed against me.

Chuckling, I hugged her to my chest. "I'll take care of him."

"This is what I need you to take care of." She rolled her hips.

I cursed and eased her off me. "Later."

She smiled.

"What?"

"I like you in Dad mode."

I frowned, easing off the bed. "Is that a thing?"

A cheeky smile curved her lips. "Oh yes. Makes me want to suck you off."

My cock jerked. I turned away, pulling on shorts and a soft tee. "Watch yourself, Ava."

"Why don't you make me, daddy?"

I turned. She wiggled her ass in the air, just begging for a spanking.

A rumbling growl left my throat and she laughed. Shaking my head, I bent and playfully tapped an ass cheek. "Sleep a little more, okay?"

I started to leave but something made me turn back.

Her left ring finger lay on a pillow, the diamond winking back at me. Warmth spread through my chest. Ava wanted me always, as I did her.

This was forever.

The feeling grew in my chest as I walked down the hallway and arrived at Wesley's room. He lit up the moment I walked through the door.

"Did you miss me?"

He made a gurgling noise, showing toothless gums.

I chuckled and picked him up from his crib. He burrowed his head against my chest, watching me with curious eyes.

"Were you expecting your mommy? She's going back to sleep."

I headed downstairs.

"Guess what? She said yes!"

Wesley smiled.

"Yes, Wes. Mommy's going to be my wife. Isn't that great?"

I flipped on a switch in the kitchen, threw open the fridge, and found a bottle of breast milk. Next to the left-overs from dinner that the Mullens had dropped off.

It'd been such a show of love since Wesley was born. Everyone Ava had helped to support. So much so that we had to turn away meals at one point.

She had worried she wouldn't be able to keep up with helping others after she gave birth. But the community rallied and kept up her program, even more joining in to show their support for the cause.

It'd been a few months since the first rush, but the help kept coming in. More diapers and baby clothes than we'd ever use sat piled up in our storage room. But for now, we were grateful for all of it.

While I heated Wesley's breakfast, I sang him a tune he didn't care for very much—if his crying was any indication.

"Milk's almost ready, okay, buddy?"

Once the bottle was warm enough, I made sure the

temperature was safe and held it to his mouth. He grabbed onto it and drank heartily.

I chuckled and exited through the back door. The deck I'd been working on was complete. Wesley and I loved our mornings out here.

And the light drizzle wouldn't bother us under the awning.

I sank into a lounge chair and held Wesley against me while I watched the rain.

"What do you think, Wes? A lovely morning? There's a whole world waiting for you, son. And you'll take it by storm."

All his attention was fixed on his bottle, not my musings.

I left him to his meal and stared out at the yard. Ava had called it the most beautiful garden she'd ever been in.

What if we had our wedding right here?

In the evenings, we loved to sit outside and enjoy a drink by the fire. It was our happy place. She moved in shortly before she had Wes and ever since, the house felt more like a home.

Nothing would bring it full circle more than saying our vows right here. I smiled at the thought. She'd just said yes and I was already planning the ceremony.

I can't believe this is my life. I was never this way before. But I loved this version of myself. And with Ava, I knew it was always going to be this way.

The back door creaked open. Then a warm hand ran over my shoulders. I tilted my head up to see Ava looking down at me.

She'd thrown a nightgown on, covering her beautiful body. Too bad. But I couldn't begrudge that.

I had her every night and always would, from here on out.

"Hey." She kissed my hair, then ran her fingers through it.

"You didn't go back to sleep?"

"Couldn't. Too excited." She flashed her ring at me.

I chuckled.

"Plus, you didn't think I'd let you enjoy this little cutie all on your own, did you?" Her eyes went to Wesley. "Hey there, little guy. How are you?"

I removed the bottle just as he smiled and reached for his mom. She collected him into her arms and then took the spot beside me.

"Did Daddy feed you breakfast? Are you happy?"

He gurgled with a big smile on his face.

"What a cutie! Yes, you are!"

Wesley put his hand in his mouth and she reached for the bottle. Our fingers brushed and her eyes met mine.

Her skin flushed and she smiled. My heart clenched. Even after having a baby and barely holding it together through endless sleepless nights, we still craved each other.

I smiled back, then reached over to push a lock of her hair behind her ear. She pressed her face into my palm before focusing on feeding Wesley.

My son. My wife-to-be. The two people I loved most in the whole world.

This wasn't the life I imagined. Not by a long shot.

But I wouldn't change a thing.

THE END

Did you like *Doctor Everything*? Then you'll LOVE *Billionaire Protector: A Grumpy Single Dad Romance*.

* * *

Keeping things professional with my grumpy, hot AF single dad boss is proving to be VERY hard...

Tattoos. Tight jeans. Fat bank account. Arrogant prick attitude.

My new boss truly has it all.

I know I shouldn't let myself get too close, but it might be too late.

He hired me as a nanny to care for his adorable boys..

But our scorching nights on the couch together after the kids go to sleep tell me he wants me to be much, much more.

I needed this job as a fresh start.

Running away from my past and starting a new life is not easy.

Especially now that my dangerous past is back to haunt me.

Like a hero, my DILF boss swoops in to protect me when no one else could.

It drives me wild and I'm falling for him hard...

I want him to claim me as his own.

I want to be free from my past.

But most of all, I want to make sure his boys are safe.

Too bad I can't have it all…or *can* I?

* * *

Start reading Billionaire Protector NOW!

Billionaire Protector
Sneak Peek

Chapter One

Violet

As soon as the elevator door shut and I glimpsed my windblown hair and flushed face in the mirrored wall, I quickly let go of my suitcase handle and reached into my purse. I powdered my cheeks and glossed my lips. Next, I ran my fingers through my hair, giving it some semblance of order. I doubted my new employer would appreciate me reporting to my new job looking like I'd just rolled out of bed after a quickie.

I looked myself over once more and sighed. Finally, I looked presentable. Why was I so worried anyway? It wasn't like I was going to work in an office. On second thought, I wish I was starting with a corporation. Then I wouldn't be so worried about what one man thought—my new boss, Shawn Hart. I'd met him and his kids once, a week ago, when he was considering me for the job. His manner was brusque, and he barely gave me two glances except when he addressed me. I was sure I didn't get the job and had already started searching job postings online when my friend and temporary roommate informed me I was mistaken.

"You got the job!" Kate bounded into her kitchen, a big grin on her face.

I choked on the sandwich I was eating and coughed before asking, "When do I start?"

"Today."

It'd taken me less than an hour to throw my few clothes into my bag, get ready, and take a cab across town. Now I was mentally preparing to start my new job as the live-in nanny to Shawn's two boys.

Before this, I was a teacher. Well-loved by my colleagues and adored by my students. A painful feeling swept through me, and I shook away the need to sulk. I left that life behind for a good reason, and this new one would be an interesting challenge. If all went according to plan, it wouldn't take long, and I could move on to bigger and better opportunities.

Now, feeling more confident, I gripped my suitcase handle and waited for the elevator to come to a stop. I stared at my face in the mirrored wall and paused. Shoot! I missed a spot. Hands shaking, I pulled out my powder. If I could just cover the circles underneath my eyes. I hadn't slept much last night because I had stayed up late job hunting. But this was no way to begin my first day, looking tired and disheveled.

The elevator jolted to a stop. I dabbed quickly, racing against time. Gah, I won't make it before the door opens. I slammed the powder case shut, started to bag it, and then paused. Standing opposite me in the open hallway was Shawn Hart. His indifferent face scanned me up and down, and his dark brows lifted.

Should I say something?

Then the elevator door began to slide shut.

I lunged forward to stop it. My powder case slipped from my grasp and clattered to the floor. *No!* I screamed internally. Turning so my back was wedged against the door, I leaned back into the elevator, dragged my bag, and picked up my powder case. I stumbled into the hallway, and the door finally slid shut.

Way to go, Violet!

My breath still came out in gasps, and it took my shaking hands a little under a minute to finally get my powder case organized and in my purse. Equilibrium slightly restored, I gazed up at my new employer.

Shawn Hart watched me with an inscrutable gaze, but I was a hundred percent certain my opinion of him was on full display. Somehow, my brain omitted the embarrassment of wrestling with the elevator and instead focused on my new boss. With every little detail my eyes took in, my heartbeat quickened.

A dark leather jacket clung to his broad chest, and black jeans hugged his muscled thighs, his outfit complete with dark shoes. If I spotted Shawn in a club, I wouldn't guess he was the father of two sons. More likely, the leader of a motorcycle club.

My eyes slid up to his face, and I had to remind myself to breathe. His blue eyes, set in a face surrounded by a dark beard and close-cropped hair, regarded me. I swallowed, unsure what to do with myself. I was tempted to tuck my hair behind my ear under his scrutiny. But that could be interpreted as flirtatious. And the last thing I needed was to invite any kind of male attention. Especially from my boss, who looked like the poster boy for the type of man any sensible woman should steer clear of. Despite this, my brain still considered all sorts of scenarios, and it took a conscious effort to stay present.

"Thanks for showing up." His deep, gruff voice filled the hallway.

The rough sound caused my belly to flip, but realization slammed into me. Was that sarcasm? Shawn didn't wait for me to respond, instead, he turned in one smooth move and crossed the carpeted hallway. I snatched my suitcase handle and followed him. He didn't glance back as he opened the apartment door and walked in. Biting my lower lip, I followed him.

Whoa.

It took a moment for my mind to appreciate the luxury around me. Everything was either white or black—at least the things that weren't kids' toys. It looked both expensive and sterile.

"I'll be gone for the rest of the day," he said.

My gaze snapped to him, and I watched him slide on a wristwatch and clip it in place.

"Your room's upstairs, the first door on the left. Food's in the kitchen." He pointed in the general direction of what I assumed was the kitchen. "Kids are in the living room. You can settle in. Just keep an ear out for them."

I nodded quickly and stayed close so I missed nothing.

We drifted into the house as he gave more instructions, and I found myself nodding before his directions even sunk in. His voice was that commanding—he left no room for questions to be asked. Once I caught myself, I shook off the fog and really listened.

But he'd stopped talking and was observing me carefully. "Do you understand?"

"Yes." Did I, though?

He walked over to an archway off the main entrance and raised his voice over the gaming sounds.

"Leon, Brady!" Somehow, he sounded less demanding.

"Yes, Dad," the kids called back.

"I'll be back a bit late, okay? Be good boys for your nanny."

"Okay, Dad," the older child called.

"Bye, Dad," the youngest said.

Any hint of softheartedness disappeared from Shawn's face as he turned to me. "They're pretty easy to deal with. They just need some guidance. Hope you can handle it."

I didn't miss how he glanced back at my bag, probably thinking of the elevator mishap. I bit back a retort and smiled stiffly instead. "I sure can, sir."

"Just Shawn." His eyes narrowed into slits.

"Of course." My smile faltered. He seemed so domineering the 'sir' thing just came out automatically.

He walked past, and I inhaled a woodsy cologne that had my body warming. I exhaled and made a mental note not to sniff my employer again. I watched him walk to the door.

Should I say goodbye? See you later? Ask when he'll be back?

The door shut as I was still contemplating it. Even though I was far away, it still felt like he slammed it in my face. I took a small step back and stared for a moment. Why did he have to be so...overbearing? Ugh, at least he was gone, and I could settle in without his brooding presence around.

I strolled through the expansive space. Without Shawn pulling all my attention, I could appreciate the decor. Everything seemed planned, and all the pieces complemented one another.

My flats barely made a sound on the marble floors that brought me to the living room. A large screen TV covered the wall, but the window view made me gasp. The kids were yelling, deep into their game, and didn't notice as I crossed the space to look out at the city.

"My goodness." The floor-to-ceiling window showcased the city in stunning detail. I pressed my face against it and did everything short of swooning. Grey buildings rose from the ground, with the blue sky and warm sun as a picturesque background.

"Are you our new nanny?"

I turned to see the boys had paused their game and were watching me curiously. The older boy, Leon, looked a lot like his dad. Dark hair and blue eyes. The younger boy, Brady, had blond hair and freckled cheeks. They were adorable.

"Yes, I am." I smiled.

"Dad's worried we won't get along," Leon said.

"Huh." I drew close to the boys. "Really? Why's that?"

"'Cause we're boys, and you're a girl."

I was twenty-eight, and it had been years since anyone called me a 'girl.' It was usually miss or ma'am, but his term made me smile anyway. "But boys and girls get along just fine."

"Girls don't play games." Leon wagged his controller at me.

I grinned. He picked the wrong *girl* to dare. "Can I try?" I stuck out a hand.

Leon and Brady glanced at each other. Brady reached out and handed me his control. It was apparent his brother had been giving him a whooping. Justice for the little one, then.

We started a new game, and it took me a little over five minutes to dwindle Leon's army down to two men. Brady stood beside me, cheering as I took the second to the last guy down, and finally, as I won.

My excitement died as I realized I had just beat a kid at

his game, but when I turned to Leon, he had a smile on his face.

"See, girls can play games, too."

"I guess," Leon said.

"Play with your brother while I settle in, ok?" I handed the device back to Brady.

The boy plopped onto the chair, excited to keep up the winning streak. I picked up my suitcase and was halfway up the stairs when I heard 'Oh, fudge brownies!' from Brady while Leon laughed out loud.

Oh, too bad for the little guy. Maybe I could find a game where he stood a chance of winning.

Once I got to the top floor, I took in the expansive corridor and doors that went down one end of the hallway and the other. Which room was the kids' and which was Shawn's? I'd probably get to know with time. I focused on letting myself into the room Shawn had directed me to.

My eyes bulged. Just like the living room, this bedroom had a breathtaking view. Not only that, the enormous space had a queen-sized bed. I strolled over to it and plopped down, rubbing the soft sheets between my fingers. Something caught my eye on the nightstand. I picked up a key and a black AMEX card. Huh. I dropped both and headed over to the window.

My head spun, looking out at the tiny hints of life in the distance. It was weird being this high up, but it was for the best. In this high-rise, my ex, Eric, couldn't get to me. He was the reason I abandoned my job and everyone I knew there, moving across the country to Cape Worth on the charity of my friends. I should probably call Kate and Layla to inform them I'd settled in, but I paused to bask in the moment.

I was free of Eric, and there was no way he'd find me here. I was a fantastic teacher, and I'd like to be just as good a nanny. My thoughts returned to my new boss. He appeared stern and unfriendly, but I didn't expect him to be chummy—just fair. A stable paycheck would allow me to save enough money to eventually live on my own and return to teaching.

I breathed deeply and let myself relax. I could do this.

Start reading Billionaire Protector NOW!

Stay in Touch

Join my Newsletter and Get a FREE Romance Book!

This is your VIP pass to a world of passion, laughter, and unputdownable stories that will make your heart race.

As a member of my newsletter family, you'll get handpicked book recommendations to keep you captivated and entertained, exclusive invites to join my ARC team, and thrilling giveaways that will make you feel like you've hit the romance jackpot!

Get Your FREE Copy of Beauty and the Grump now!

It's a a tantalizing brother's best friend romance that will leave you breathless and begging for more.

———

Billionaire. Ranch owner. Single dad.

And now this infuriatingly hot bull-riding grump is my boss.

All I have to do is care for his adorably wild 6-year-old son until he can find a new full-time nanny.

Easier said than done…

Resisting the urge to touch this arrogant DILf's body long enough for me to make money so I can move back to the city seems basically impossible.

But when he spitefully offered me a huge bonus - enough for me to get out of here and back to the city - I couldn't say no.

We have to keep things professional at all costs.

This "country way of life" is going to kill me. Literally.

Now the worst tornado of the century is overhead and we're trapped in a storm cellar together.

We have no choice but to get close. Real close.

There are only two things that can happen now that we're stuck together:

Hold up this professional charade or let him have his way with me…

Get Your FREE Copy of Beauty and the Grump now!

https://geni.us/ebnewsletter

Made in United States
Orlando, FL
26 August 2024

50797410R00137